MR. WILDER

MR. WILDER

A NOVEL

Shelton R. Johnson

Cover illustration and design provided by Ms. Camile Maddow.
ISBN: 0692937501
ISBN 13: 9780692937501

*Registered with the Writer's Guild of America, East.

Dedicated with love to Danielle, Nadia, and Jack. It is my prayer that this book will bring an end to the racial divide in this great country that I call home and initiate a global desire for world peace.

Also By Shelton R. Johnson

Books

Thankful for My Family: A Thanksgiving Comedy (I of III)

Merry with My Family: A Christmas Comedy (II of III)

In the Works

A New Year's Comedy (III of III)

"We're not talking about a fucking animal here, lady! We're talking about a teenage boy! A good teenage boy! A straight-A student! Shot and killed in cold blood by a teacher that you hired!" The homely looking woman stood and shouted among the seated but rowdy crowd of parents in the auditorium. The woman onstage stood in solitude except for the mayor, who stood ten yards away from her with his head down, texting and laughing. His robust stomach shook up and down with each chuckle.

"Ma'am, I'm very aware of the situation at hand," the woman said nervously as she gripped the sides of the podium with her sweaty palms, causing her otherwise-pasty fists to turn red.

An elderly man who sat up front with a white beard slowly rose to speak as the shouting crowd became silent to listen. "I'm not so sure that you do, miss principal lady. See, I reads the paper. I know they brought you on board last year straight out of college. I also know that the board of education gave you $75,000 to update the surveillance system in the school. So why haven't we seen those yet?" The mayor quickly put his phone away while looking at the crowd with fearful, bulging eyes as he hesitated to cough. The pissed-off African American parents who filled the auditorium and flowed out into the hallway began to chant, with fists balled in the air, "Show us the film! Show us the film! Show us the film!"

The principal, who hadn't changed her posture behind the podium, was visibly shaken. Her necklace, which covered the purple blouse beneath her gray blazer, began to rattle as she spoke into the microphone. "In an effort to expedite the investigation, I have submitted all surveillance material and the personal information of both the teacher and student over to the local law enforcement." The elderly man remained standing as a parent yelled, "They ain't gonna do shit! The police haven't even arrested the motherfucker yet!" Parents blurted out verbal affirmations at will.

A large woman who sat next to the wall stood to speak while using her arms to clinch her purse tightly against her pea coat. "I just want to say that I blame all this stuff on you, lady!" The woman pointed in the principal's direction. "If you would have had some extracurricular activities for the kids to do, this might not have happened! All y'all have is sports! So I guess a nonathletic person is just supposed to get shot and killed while he waits for his grandmother to pick him up, huh?" The room was in an uproar as the woman took her seat.

The mayor walked closer to the podium while adjusting his suit jacket as the elderly man in the front raised his lengthy arm to silence the crowd. "Listen to me, miss principal lady—"

The principal cut him off with agitated tone. "Akers, sir. My name is Ms. Akers." She then pointed to her engagement ring with a smile, saying, "And soon to be Mrs."

The elderly man paused to look up at her before snatching his glasses off. "Heffa, I don't give a——" His wife tugged at his pant leg to stop him. The smile immediately left Principal Akers's face. The elderly man regathered his thoughts and composure as he put his glasses back on. "Listen to me, *Miss Akers*, almost every month around this country, a black person is killed by a white person. And the white person always gets little or no consequence. Now, if you think I'm going to let that crap happen in my hometown of Norfolk, Virginia, where I've lived for eighty-one years, you and that mayor got another thing coming. I will take the little bit of life I have left to see to it that that teacher of yours gets what he deserves." The crowd cheered the elderly man on as the mayor and Principal Akers stood silently while slowly nodding. He gradually raised his hand again. The wooden fold-down chairs began to squeak as most of the parents took their seats.

"Let me ask you something, Ms. Akers." The elderly man spoke as the mayor patted his rosy red cheeks and forehead dry with his handkerchief. "As the principal, you're in charge of the hiring and firing of the teachers, correct?"

Ms. Akers quickly responded, "I'm in charge of the hiring and, unfortunately, the firing of all staff, sir, including cafeteria and janitorial staff."

The man held two fingers on his chin as he nodded, mumbling, "Very good, very good." He looked up to ask, "Now, did you fire the teacher who killed LaVeon Kirkland?"

Ms. Akers rapidly responded a second time. "Yes, I did. Immediately."

The parents gave an ovation as the elderly man continued to look down, nodding. "Very good. Very good." The crowd became silent once again. "We know you've only been here for a year, and you hired him. I'm interested to know, though, how many teachers you have hired in your time as principal."

Ms. Akers stuck her already-large chest out to answer. "I'm proud to say that I have had the pleasure of hiring fifteen new teachers in my time here at Booker T. Washington High School. Last summer, I had ten teachers retire and hired fifteen to improve the student-to-teacher ratio, bringing my teaching staff to seventy." Although there were a few claps, there were a lot of head nods in the crowd and a large grin from the mayor and proud principal.

The elderly man clapped leisurely. "Very good. Very good." He stopped to ask, "Now, as I said before, I reads the paper. So I know that six of those teachers who retired were black, and you hired fifteen more white teachers to your already-all-white teaching staff. I'll get to the point. My question is, if all the janitors are black, all the cafeteria workers are black, your student population is 98 percent black, and you have a black college two minutes up the road, Norfolk State University, how and why do you have an all-white faculty with no repercussions from the board of education?"

Principal Akers gasped as her eyes flared open like a deer in headlights. Everyone in the crowd stood up, shouting out individual demands for better education and equal job opportunities.

Officer Timmons stood at the top of the stairs leading to the stage. He was a jittery, frail-bodied police officer with a thick white mustache and even thicker eyeglasses that covered his wrinkled cocoa-brown skin. He adjusted his service belt with both hands before reaching back to put his hand on his gun while mumbling under his breath, "Y'all better sit y'all ass down. I'll shoot everybody in this motherfucker."

"Excuse me!" Principal Akers exclaimed. "I don't see color."

A slender woman near the front had a voice that rose above the rest. "We know you don't see color, little miss thang! Why in the hell do you think we're here? We're sick of you only seeing white!" The woman's comments caused the unruly crowd to grow even stronger.

The mayor nearly ripped the back off his suit jacket as he reached for the microphone with his stubby arms. With panic in his voice, he said, "I do apologize. That is all the time we have. If you have any further questions, please feel free to visit our website. Thank you all for coming out, and have a good night!" The crowd began to boo as the mayor turned to wrap his arm around Principal Akers and walked her behind the curtains. She had her back turned to the crowd and her head resting in her hands as tears flowed down her face, causing makeup to drip on her black high-heeled shoes.

A lady in the front row threw one of her shoes at the mayor's back, but it fell short as the elderly man continued to argue. "Not only did you not receive any repercussions, they gave you an additional $75,000 for fuckin' surveillance! What's wrong? You scared of black people, so you need to watch us? Y'all are the ones killing our children! We need to be watching y'all! We've been needing new computers in the library for eight years! That's a $10,000 fix, and they haven't sent diddly squat!

I guess your white teachers' safety is more important than our black students' edu-fuckin-cation!"

The mayor and Principal Akers were behind the closed curtain. The feisty parents began to exit the high school's auditorium through the double doors. Still in saddened shock, Principal Akers sniffled. Her tears continued to flow with the mayor's arm around her shoulders. "I can't believe this. I just can't believe this. I've never been accused of being a racist my whole life. Hell, I grew up in Detroit." Principal Akers took a step away from the mayor to look him in the eye. "You know, I really meant what I said up there. I really don't see color." The mayor nodded rapidly as he reached in the interior pocket of his suit jacket to hand her his spare handkerchief, making light of the fact that he was a heavy sweater. "Those teachers I hired were the best that I could find for the budget and positions available. I didn't know that being local and being black was something that I needed to factor into my evaluation process. Besides, who would want to do that, anyway? When I was in college, anyone who lived in the city and wasn't a student was called a 'townie.' And, let me tell you, that was not a cool thing to be."

The mayor looked around to confirm that there was no one listening in on their conversation before he spoke. "Listen, Kirsten, you don't have to explain it to me. This is just another case where one redneck goes and does something stupid. Now all the blacks think every white person in a position of authority is a discrete member of the Ku Klux Klan."

Principal Akers explained, "Yes, but Mr. Schmidt wasn't like that. He even let the students call him by his first name, Riley. He was popular among the teachers too. He was the type who'd always make you laugh when you spoke to him."

The mayor sighed deeply before politely speaking, his Boston accent was strong. "Either way, what's done is done. And Mr. Schmidt should not have killed that boy. Now, unfortunately, that old geezer out there was right. These white-on-black murders have been taking place quite often in the past year or so." The mayor waved his hand around as he continued to speak carelessly.

"What usually happens is the blacks get all riled up like you saw tonight. Then, they might march or have some church members come pray your ass to death, or, God forbid, both. If news reporters show up, you just keep your answers generic, and, in about a year or so, everything will be back to normal."

Principal Akers looked up at the mayor in shock with the handkerchief covering her mouth. "Aww, don't look so worried, Kirsten. You'll do just fine. All I can say is welcome to Norfolk Public Schools. You know your dad and I are old navy buddies. So when he called saying you wanted a principal's position, I warned him that this was the only one I had available, and you insisted. Now, here we are."

Principal Akers nodded in agreement. "Yeah, here we are."

The mayor wrapped his arms around her for comfort. "Kirsten, listen. It's not that bad. You did a good job in firing that teacher as soon as you heard the news. Look at how all the blacks cheered for that. So they know that you have at least some decency. If you really want to show them you care, do what the fat lady said. Set up an extracurricular activity for the kids after school. Nobody will care, but it will be good for the blacks to see that you're trying."

Principal Akers perked up. "Yeah. You know what? I'll do that. I think I know just the thing too."

The mayor responded as he began to walk away, the heels of his brown dress shoes causing a clicking sound with each step on the hardwood floor. "Well, good. Don't be too hard on yourself, and keep me posted on how it goes."

Principal Akers quickly raised her hand as she blurted out, "Wait a second, Mayor Newman!"

He turned around with a grin. "Please, just call me Rich. It's what your dad calls me."

They both chuckled prior to Principal Akers wondering aloud, "When will I be getting the new computers for the library?"

Mayor Newman looked down briefly before raising his head with a smile. "Listen. Granby High school is fifteen minutes up the road in the middle of a Jewish neighborhood. Last year, the *y* and the *m* went missing from the word 'gymnasium' that hung outside the school's athletic area. Yeah, I heard about it, and it was only a $300 fix. But I figured, who cares? It's only two freakin' letters! Do you want to know how many complaint letters I received?" Principal Akers had a blank look on her face. "Seven hundred eighty freakin' letters! There are only six hundred people in the community! I said okay—I'll handle it. But I drug my feet. The letters started going up the chain to congress and to the senate. Then, I made it a priority and had it fixed that week." Principal Akers squinted her eyes in confusion.

"I said that to say this. It's not about race. That community did what they had to do to get what they wanted, and they weren't going to be ignored or put off to the side. Now you have one black senior citizen who shouts out a request for computers at a meeting that's supposed to be about a student being killed by a teacher last week. No! It doesn't work that way. I haven't heard anything about those computers in almost five years. That's why I say the blacks only come together when they feel like they've been mistreated. And even then, they don't do what is necessary to get the things they want.

"So it's our job to pat them on the ass, tell them what they want to hear, and then go about our business." Principal Akers's pupils were fully exposed as she took a step back in disbelief of what she had just heard from Mayor Newman. "Listen, kid, I admire your desire to improve things around here. But you'll learn, just like I did, the blacks don't want to improve themselves. In the meantime, let me worry about where the school's budget goes. You just enjoy that new security system, and get started on your extracurricular activity." Before exiting, the mayor turned to ask, "Do you know what NAACP stands for?"

Principal Akers responded, "It's a minority support group."

She was corrected. "It stands for the National Association for the Advancement of Colored People. Here's my question to you though, and I don't want you to answer—it's just food for thought. Where is the 'advancement' if the only time you see them is after a tragedy?"

—⟨∞⟩—

Two days later, there was a cool autumn breeze that filled the air, perfect for the high school's football team, who'd be playing their first game of the season that night. Suddenly, without braking, an old, dinged-up Chevy Lumina crashed onto the ramp and sped into a fully occupied parking lot. With the windows rolled down, the driver's music, "Cocaine" by Eric Clapton, played loud enough to be heard throughout the bricked-in school. The car swung into a vacant handicap spot. The cement paver was the only thing that stopped its forward momentum. The driver reached into a clutter-filled back seat in search of a handicap sticker. Without warning, after the driver slapped the wrinkled, grease-stained sticker onto the rear-view mirror, the driver's door flew open. Feet first, displaying mismatched socks, a man got out of the vehicle with a cane in one hand and a business portfolio in the other.

He used his hip to bump the car door shut before a hissing sound grabbed his attention, causing him to look down at his tire. The front driver-side tire had a shattered beer bottle beneath it. "Who the fuck would leave an empty beer bottle in a handicap spot at a high school?" the man thought aloud. He bent over slightly to take a closer look and then popped back up after getting a whiff of urine. "Punk bastards!" he shouted before checking his watch and rushing inside the main entrance between the large white columns. Even with the cane, the middle-aged man had an obvious limp in his left leg.

Once inside, his worn-down dress shoes didn't make a sound as he rushed across the ceramic floor in the foyer on his way to the front office.

Principal Akers wore a beige skirt suit. She greeted him with a handshake and a reciprocated, exceptionally large smile. "Hi, sir. I'm Principal Akers. How can I help you?" He was so focused on her massive, protruding breasts, which tested the strength of the buttons on her blazer, that he didn't even notice Principal Akers's long, wavy brunette hair, red lipstick, and sky-blue eyes. He also didn't notice the fact that she'd asked him a question.

The man placed his portfolio on top of the laminate counter in between them. "Huh? Oh, um, yes, yes. I have an interview set up with you for two thirty."

She responded, "Oh, you're my two thirty? You're late."

He began to mumble through excuses before the principal raised her right hand and pressed the button to allow the man to walk behind the counter. "It's okay. Just follow me to my office," Principal Akers said. While walking directly behind her, the man noticed the high-heeled shoes beneath her long, athletically toned legs leading up to a shapely posterior. He thought, "Nice ass." A gentleman in regards, he spoke to everyone in the front office before closing the principal's office door behind himself.

"Please, have a seat," Principal Akers insisted as she extended her arm toward the two pub-style chairs across from her desk. "So you made it through our background check rather fast. That's a good thing. I've also taken the time to read your resume and noticed that you've written fifteen books." She stopped to look up and noticed him staring at her breasts. After making eye contact, he sat up in his seat and used his bold, authoritative voice to explain how the glare from the sunlight bursting through the window behind her was getting in his eye. The man began to rub his thick, straggly, brunette-and-gray goatee as Principal Akers reached back to close the blinds. During that time, he took the liberty of glancing at the wall and noticed her bachelor's and master's certificates, both from the University of Delaware. Beneath them, a group picture with her friends in what looked like a bar or nightclub hung on the wall.

The gentleman asked, "Where was that taken?"

She quickly responded with a smile. "Oh, that was at my engagement party after my fiancé proposed."

He could hardly see the mustard seed-sized diamond she pointed to with such enthusiasm. Curious as to whether or not he had a chance with Principal Akers, the man commented, "So you found your soul mate, huh?"

She responded sternly, "Absolutely. I couldn't imagine spending my life with anyone else. He's just a good man, and let me tell you, they're not easy to come by." He scratched his head, which was bald on the top, with the same color hair as his goatee along the sides.

She rolled away from her desk to stand. "Well, we need to get the ball rolling here, sir. It's 3:05 p.m., and the bell that releases the students will be ringing in a minute." The two shook hands and made eye contact as Principal Akers said, "Congratulations, Mr. Wilder. You've got the job. It's every Tuesday for two hours after school, and it pays one hundred dollars a week." Mr. Wilder quickly stood up to thank her and questioned her hasty decision. She replied using hand gestures. "Look, you're the only one who applied, and, quite frankly, this whole 'extracurricular activity' thing is just something I put in place to earn some cool points with the black community, since one of my best students, LaVeon, was killed by one of our staff members last week."

Mr. Wilder nodded his head. "Yeah, I heard about that."

Principal Akers quickly blurted out, "Now, don't go thinking I'm some racist, because I'm not. That couldn't be further from the truth. I just learned at the last meeting with the parents that no matter what I do, it won't suffice. So I'm just going to answer their requests the best I can and keep it moving."

Mr. Wilder said, "Look, you don't have to explain racism to me. I grew up in Danville, Virginia, where there's more Confederate flags than jobs. But do you think hiring another white instructor is a smart move?"

She shrugged her shoulders. "Like I said, you're the only one who applied…and why did you apply, sir?"

He gazed into the principal's eyes as he spoke. "Well, I've always cared about the youth. I do believe they are our future. And literature is a great—"

"I've already offered you the job, Mr. Wilder," Principal Akers interrupted as she stared back at him with a grin.

"Okay. I could use the extra cash."

Principal Akers nodded as she thought, "Fair enough."

She opened the door, and Mr. Wilder stopped to ask, "Why creative writing?" Without hesitation, she answered, "It's what I did when I was younger. I enjoyed it, because it was a judgment-free way for me to express myself. I figured it might serve my students in the same manner."

The school bell rang as the two began to exit Principal Akers's office. The students' footsteps above the main office sounded like hail falling on the roof of a car in that aged building. Suddenly, through the glass wall that looked out into the main entry foyer, there was an influx of anxious students that trampled the hallway to go home. As she grabbed her jacket off the wooden coatrack and reached for one of the security walkie-talkies on the counter, Principal Akers said, "Mr. Wilder, you might want to just have a seat in here for a bit until the hallways clear. These teenagers won't have any patience to wait on a seasoned man with a cane." He took her advice as he adjusted the necktie beneath his V neck sweater and suit jacket before flopping down on the end of the couch.

At the other end of the couch, asleep, sat the police officer who regularly worked security detail. Principal Akers was on her way out into the hallway when she noticed him sleeping and shouted, "Officer Timmons! Officer Timmons!" He groggily sat up, and his eyes popped open as he used his forearm to wipe the drool off his lips. She continued as she threw a walkie-talkie in his lap. "Wake up! It's the end of the school day. I need you out in the main foyer." Officer Timmons sat and stared at her for a few seconds before rolling his eyes and rubbing his mustache as he stood up and slowly walked out. Principal Akers followed closely behind. Because of his petite stature, Officer Timmons was difficult to notice in the herd of students.

Mr. Wilder stood up, leaned against the front counter, and used the phone to call a tow truck for his car. Mr. Wilder was a large man. He stood nearly six foot four with broad shoulders and long arms. Even with the cane serving as proof of his lack of mobility, he showed no pudge of the stomach. In fact, he had a solid thickness about him, as if he were not a stranger to physical labor.

A man with a strong hillbilly accent answered on the other end of the phone. "Mickey's Tow Service. If you've got the bucks, we've got the trucks. This is Little Mickey speaking. Who do I have the pleasure of speaking with today?"

"Hi, my name is Brett Wilder. I need my '98 Chevy Lumina towed from Booker T. Washington High School on Virginia Beach Boulevard. Do you know where that is?"

"No, sir. I can't rightfully say that I do. The last person in our family to graduate from high school was my daddy, Big Mickey, and he's on the shitter right now. I should be able to find it on my GPS, though." Mr. Wilder dropped his head and shook it in disbelief. "Now, what seems to be the problem wit' ya car, Mister...uh...Wilder?"

"Nothing's wrong with the car. I just got a flat tire after I drove over a bottle of piss in the parking lot."

"All right, sir. Well, that will be $115, and I will be there in less than an hour."

Mr. Wilder stood erect. "Whoa! I saw your ad in the paper that said all tows are one hundred dollars."

"Yes, sir, but that didn't take into account the fifteen-dollar piss fee."

"Wait a minute. You can't start charging fees at your own convenience, Little Mickey! Do we need to talk to Big Mickey about this?"

"Nope. No, sir. There's no need to drag my pa off the shitter for this one. My gloves cost fifteen dollars, and there's a really good chance that I'll end up gettin' some piss on 'em and needing to replace 'em. So there you have the creation of the fifteen-dollar piss fee."

Boom! A loud thump came from the glass wall as Officer Timmons's body was shoved up against it. As Mr. Wilder turned to see what was going on, he could hear Principal Akers over the spare security walky-talky on the counter. "Security! We have a fight in the main foyer!"

Mr. Wilder yelled at the young hillbilly on the phone. "Whatever! I'll pay the piss fee! Just get here!" He hung up the phone, threw his cane on the couch, and hastily skipped out into the foyer full of students standing around watching. Principal Akers was no different as she stood as far away as the school's walls would allow, gripping her walky-talky with both hands. Mr. Wilder used his lengthy arms to grab both teenage boys by the collars and separate them, allowing Officer Timmons to step away from the wall.

There was an obvious height difference between the two young men. Officer Timmons grabbed the smallest by the neck and immediately began to trash-talk the onlooking students as he and Mr. Wilder escorted the two boys into the main office.

"Yeah! Y'all students just learned a valuable lesson! Don't put your hands on ol' Officer Timmons! I'm 125 pounds of trouble, motherfucker!" He adjusted his impervious glasses before continuing to speak. "That's right! I'll shoot everybody in this damn school!"

Mr. Wilder became irritated as they approached the main office door. "Hey, Officer, why don't you calm down? These are kids you're talking to."

Officer Timmons and the young man who's neck the officer had his arm around both stopped to look up at Mr. Wilder. They pulled their heads back in shock. Out of nowhere, Principal Akers grabbed Mr. Wilder's arm and opened the office door to allow the four of them in as she whispered in his ear, "Listen. Let's not get Officer Timmons any more riled up than he already is. Even with his overly medicated glasses, he can hardly see anything. So if he does pull out his gun, he *will* shoot everybody in here."

Mr. Wilder cut his eyes at her as she walked away, thinking, "Thanks for the tip."

The teenage boys sat on opposite ends of the couch, pleading their cases while Officer Timmons sat between them. The smaller one asked, "I don't know why I'm in here, anyway! Y'all know Jaylen stay angry about something!"

The taller boy responded, "What? This won't my fault! Ms. Akers, you know CJ got that big mouth he don't know how to shut!"

CJ, the shorter teenage boy, quickly sat up in his seat to argue. "I told you, stop calling me that! My name is Curtis, you ol' pear-shaped-face-having boy. Yo' high yellow ass sitting over there looking like undeveloped sperm."

Officer Timmons burst into laughter and then caught himself before giving Curtis credit. "That was a good one, boy."

Jaylen's ears were getting redder by the second. "That's all right. Go ahead, and laugh it up. When I catch you in the hallway, your ass is mine."

Quick witted, Curtis responded, "Wow, Jaylen, I'm proud of you for coming out the way you did. But I need to tell you that I don't participate in homosexual activities."

Jaylen's snapped his head back, offended. "What? I'm not gay!"

"I don't know about that. You said if you see me in the hallway, you're going to want my ass. And if it's all the same to you, I'd like to keep my ass out of this. I mean, you can fight me if you'd like. But I want to keep my ass limited to washcloths and toilet seats."

Principal Akers shook her head with pouty lips as Mr. Wilder chuckled briefly. Officer Timmons was holding his stomach with his head leaned back on the couch, laughing hysterically. "That boy a fool!"

Jaylen yelled over Officer Timmons, exposing the veins in his neck. "Man, kiss my ass!"

With a smile, Curtis replied, "Look, Jaylen, we all know you just came out the closet. But that don't mean that you have to start bombarding us with your gay requests."

Now with his fists balled and pressed against his knees, Jaylen shouted, "Fuck you, CJ!"

The smile quickly left Curtis's face as he used his right index finger to point at Jaylen's eyes. "I told you to stop calling me that shit!" Officer Timmons slapped Curtis's hand down before using his arms and body to keep the two separated.

Principal Akers stepped in. "That's enough! Neither one of you needs to be worried about being seen in the hallways, because you're both suspended." Curtis and Jaylen carried on griping as Principal Akers separated the two by asking Curtis to go sit in her office.

During that time, Mr. Wilder had noticed a tall young man walk in through the rear entry of the main office. He had put his stuffed book bag down and immediately begun organizing the unwieldy stack of folders on the wooden desk closest to the back wall. After Principal Akers closed her office door behind Curtis, Officer Timmons looked up and noticed the boy. "You don't take no days off, do you, boy?" he blurted across the office. The awkwardly thin teenager in loose-fitting, worn-down clothes bashfully smiled without looking up to acknowledge Officer Timmons.

The phone on the counter rang. Principal Akers answered and notified Mr. Wilder that it was Mickey's Tow Service calling to say they were outside.

"Okay, thank you. It seems like everything is under control here. I'll see you Tuesday after school. Thanks again."

Principle Akers replied, "No. Thank you, sir. And I apologize for everything that took place this afternoon."

"Not a problem at all, ma'am."

Officer Timmons mumbled under his breath, "I know she didn't just hire another white man. This heffa couldn't catch a clue if it had duct tape on it. Forget these kids, I might have to shoot her ass."

Mr. Wilder said, "Excuse me, young man, can you hand me my cane next to your leg?" Jaylen, who wore a white, V neck T-shirt, saw Mr. Wilder's cane leaning against his gray sweatpants and said, "Get it yourself, white man," while looking him in the eyes.

Mr. Wilder's eyes suddenly narrowed with rage as Principal Akers spoke up. "Please ignore him, Mr. Wilder. He's always angry about something. Jaylen, give the gentleman his cane like he asked before I have to start making phone calls."

Jaylen raised one of his new sneakers off the floor and kicked the cane down in Mr. Wilder's direction. Jaylen and Mr. Wilder continued to stare into each other's eyes as he bent over to pick up his cane. He exited the office.

Once in the parking lot, he was greeted with a bill from Little Mickey, a large, bearded, redhead man wearing overalls and a sweaty tow service baseball cap. It took Mr. Wilder a good amount of time to dig through his back seat for his checkbook. Once the bill was paid, Mr. Wilder sat in the tow truck, which had a broken radio, forcing him to listen to Little Mickey sing more Charlie Daniels songs than any self-respecting Georgian would care to hear. While stopped at the red light in front of the school, Mr. Wilder noticed the thin young man from the back of the office leaving the school through the cafeteria doors. With his attention sparked, Mr. Wilder sat up in his seat to watch the young man say good-bye to the janitors. He then walked unusually close to the dumpsters before swiftly changing his direction toward the underpass behind the school. It was as if he'd forgotten which way he was supposed to go. The light turned green, and they pulled away. Mr. Wilder scratched his head in wonder.

The following Tuesday, at three fifteen sharp, Mr. Wilder walked into the high school's front office. He wore his typical collared shirt and tie covered by a V neck sweater and blazer. The hallways were essentially clear with the exception of a few stragglers who had missed their bus. Principal Akers was standing behind the counter waiting on him. After a brief greeting, Principal Akers handed him a small stack of papers to sign.

As Mr. Wilder filled out the necessary forms, he peeked up to ask, "Who was that young man in here on Friday who stayed in the back, organizing?"

A smile came over Principal Akers's face. "That was DeSean. He's one of our best students, and he's a hard worker too. He helps us out a lot in the front office and library. I give him a little cash on Fridays when I can afford to, because he does such a good job. I don't know where this office would be without him. Why'd you ask?"

Mr. Wilder had finished with the papers and slowly pushed them back over to Principal Akers. He looked her in the eyes to answer. "No reason. I noticed him leaving, and he seemed a bit lost, is all."

Principal Akers snatched the papers off the counter, turned her back to Mr. Wilder, and answered hastily while putting them away. "That's odd. I don't know why DeSean would seem lost. Either way, you can go see Officer Timmons out in the hallway, and he will show you to your classroom."

Mr. Wilder squinted his eyes, questioning why she never turned back around to look at him. As opposed to asking, he decided to follow her instructions.

"Hey, polar bear!" Officer Timmons shouted across the hallway to Mr. Wilder. He walked toward Mr. Wilder, giggling in his loose-fitting uniform with his thumbs tucked behind his service belt. "The last time I saw something big and white like you, I had to take out a mortgage." After noticing Mr. Wilder wasn't laughing along with him, Officer Timmons pulled himself together. "Hey, loosen up, man. You're going to have to learn how to take a joke if you're going to be working around here."

Mr. Wilder asked, "So threatening to shoot everyone is your way of joking?"

Officer Timmons's raised his eyebrows. He rested one hand on his protruding stomach and the other in the air to politely disrupt Mr. Wilder. "Whoa! Whoa! Whoa! Let's back this up a bit. I think we got off on the wrong foot." Officer Timmons stuck out his hand. "The name is Gary Timmons. Everybody around here just calls me Officer Timmons. I work security detail for the City of Norfolk Police Department."

Mr. Wilder nodded slowly as he reached to shake Officer Timmons's hand while looking him in the eyes, which was hard to do considering the thickness of his lenses. "Brett Wilder. Part-time creative writing teacher." The two began to walk down the hallway.

"Listen, I know it might sound harsh with me threatening to shoot and all. But you should know that I've been in law enforcement for almost forty years and have never even drawn my weapon. I became an officer to help people, not hurt them. Now, as far as these kids are concerned, if they think that you're soft, they'll run all over you. And, as you can see, I'm not the most physically intimidating fella'. So I say what I know works. But they don't know that I would give my life in a moment's notice for any one of them."

"That's good to know, Officer Timmons. Thanks for sharing that with me. It looks like I'm at my room now, so I'll be heading in. Thanks again."

Officer Timmons squinted his eyes and tilted his head, trying to read Mr. Wilder before he entered his classroom. Abruptly, Officer

Timmons said, "Hey. Hold on a minute. You're not one of those crazy white boys like Riley was, are you? Smile in my face and then run off and put a bullet in one of the best kids in here?"

Mr. Wilder didn't hesitate to respond, his face scrunched in shock. "No, sir. I'm not like that at all." Mr. Wilder turned away as Officer Timmons nodded.

"Good. Good. Because if I ever see Riley Schmidt again, that's one person I will shoot and won't think twice about it. I still can't believe he did it. LaVeon was such a good kid."

Mr. Wilder agreed. "Yes, Principal Akers was telling me."

"He was smart too, and knew his math. That boy was so good at math, I let him do my taxes."

Mr. Wilder interrupted him. "What? You let a high school student file your taxes?"

Officer Timmons eyed Mr. Wilder down and back up again. "Shit yeah! I got a return that year too. Now I got to go back to my wife's sister to get mine done, and hear her mouth. '*Why y'all ain't paying your tithes? Why y'all still got separate accounts? You can't claim your grandson just because you babysit him all the time.*' Ain't nobody trying to hear all that shit!"

Mr. Wilder chuckled for a bit. "I really should get going so I can set up."

Officer Timmons waved him off. "Oh yeah, yeah. Go ahead, Mr. Wilder. Sorry for rambling on like that. Have a good evening."

Mr. Wilder hurried past the heavy, wooden door into the classroom. He anticipated an influx of students eager to see what this new creative writing thing was all about. He found a broken piece of chalk alongside the blackboard and wrote, in big, cursive letters, "Creative Writing." He then sat in the teacher's chair and tapped his fingers on the desk. Mr. Wilder watched the narrow window above the door knob for potential students.

The time was five thirty, which meant quitting time for Mr. Wilder. Not a single student had showed up. Principal Akers didn't even come to check in and see how things were going. After erasing what he'd written on the board, Mr. Wilder grabbed his business portfolio. While looking at a room full of chairs with fold-up desks, he thought to himself, "That was the easiest hundred I've ever made." That feeling was short-lived, though. As Mr. Wilder walked down the poorly lit hallway with burgundy lockers and dingy, beige flooring, he began to doubt whether there was truly a need for him to be there. He also thought about things he could do to bring students in.

Outside, it was nearly dark as Mr. Wilder noticed the parking lot lights flicker. After putting his key in the door, Mr. Wilder looked back at the school and saw one of the more senior janitors staring at him as he shook out the welcome mats. Mr. Wilder briefly made eye contact with him before the tall janitor looked away and focused on the mats. Mr. Wilder didn't scratch his head long to wonder what the janitor may have been staring at. He just shrugged his shoulders, hopped in his car, and drove off.

———oᏏᏏᏕ———

Exactly one week later, at three fifteen on the dot, Mr. Wilder entered Booker T. Washington High School. He walked straight to his classroom with a slight grin. After getting everything set up, he pulled out a portable cassette player and began to play Led Zeppelin's greatest hits. Mr. Wilder thought, "These are teenagers, so they have to love music. This will at least get them to my door. I can talk them in from there." He propped the classroom door as wide as it could go. The oversized windows overlooking the apartments across the street illuminated the classroom and a good portion of the hallway beyond the door.

Thirty minutes passed. Mr. Wilder sat with his feet crossed on the desk, leaning back with his fingers locked behind his head. Led Zeppelin's "Night Flight" was playing on the cassette player. Over the music he heard an argument going on out in the hallway that made him sit up in his chair. Mr. Wilder grabbed his cane, but before he could even use it to stand, Officer Timmons, Curtis, and Jaylen were standing in his doorway.

"Hey, Mr. Wilder. I figured you could use these two students in your classroom," Officer Timmons said while looking Mr. Wilder in the eyes.

Mr. Wilder stood up and rushed over to greet him with an enthusiastic handshake. "Absolutely. Absolutely."

"Yeah, they were both in in-school suspension arguing about some raps or poems they had wrote. Neither one of them had somewhere they needed to be immediately after school. So I thought this might be a good place for them to come."

Mr. Wilder agreed. "Yes, come in. Have a seat wherever you'd like."

Jaylen slowly took a few steps and sat at the desk closest to the door. Curtis argued, "I ain't sitting in this classroom with that wack-ass music playing. I'm popular! I got a reputation to keep." Jaylen rolled his eyes and dropped his head in his hands.

Officer Timmons shoved Curtis in the back. "What? Curtis, you 'bout as popular as an ice cream truck in a snowstorm. Boy, go sit your simple ass down in one of those seats." Curtis reluctantly walked to the seat up front, closest to the window. Officer Timmons stood there scratching his head full of gray hair. Mr. Wilder hurried over to turn off his cassette player.

After rubbing his fresh, bald fade, Curtis turned to face Officer Timmons in new tennis shoes, denim jeans, and a red polo which still had the factory fold lines. "Okay. I'm only doing this for you, though, Officer Timmons, 'cause you my dude. But don't think for one second that I'm just gonna let you get away with joking me like that, with all that thick white facial hair you got. Lookin' like a black Willie Nelson."

Officer Timmons's eyes opened wide in shock. "Oh, you know better than to mess with me, you ol' zit-poppin', cauliflower-face-having, whole-bottle-of-Neutrogena-using juvenile."

Curtis smiled as he nodded. "That's okay. At least I can make it to the bathroom in time to use it. That's more than I can say for you, you ol' penguin-pace-walkin' senior citizen."

Mr. Wilder put both of his hands in the air. "All right! That's enough!" Jaylen's forehead and throat were red from laughing so hard. Mr. Wilder even had a smirk on his face.

Officer Timmons concurred. "He's right. That is enough. Now, y'all boys mind your manners with Mr. Wilder here. And don't give him no trouble. If I get a call about somebody acting up, I'll come down here and—"

"Shoot everybody. We know. We know." Jaylen and Curtis finished his sentence in unison.

"That's right. I'll shoot every last one of y'all."

Curtis scrunched his face and said, "It ain't but two of us, though, Officer Timmons. Why'd you say 'every last one of y'all' like we're a lot of people?"

"Boy, shut your ass up! Don't get smart with me! I already graduated high school. I know how to count." Officer Timmons closed the door behind himself as he exited the classroom.

Mr. Wilder sat on his desk and asked, "So tell me about this rap poem you guys created."

Curtis jerked his neck and used his thumb to point toward Jaylen. "Man, it ain't no rap poem. I wrote a rap, and he wrote some gay-ass poem."

Jaylen asked, "How is it gay if I wrote it for a girl, CJ?"

Curtis slapped his hand down on the desk in anger before pointing at Jaylen. "Boy, you lucky Timmons said don't start nothin'! Or I'd be over there whippin' your ass right now!"

Jaylen pretended to yawn with his hands in his pockets. "Yeah, more like gettin' your lil' ass whipped right now, Curtis Jordan Jr."

Curtis stood up at his desk, speaking with contempt in his high-pitched voice. "A, yo, teach! You better get yo' boy, and tell him cut out all that junior shit!"

Mr. Wilder spoke up. "All right, that's enough of that!"

With hostility, Jaylen squinted his eyes. "I don't see why? Everybody been calling him CJ since the third grade. Now, all of a sudden, he wants to snap on people who don't call him Curtis."

Mr. Wilder said, "Okay, never mind all that, though. Tell me more about this poem you wrote."

Still hostile, Jaylen answered, "For what, white man? You wanna steal that too? I know your history. Every time a black person creates something, or finds something good, you either steal it or kill it!"

Mr. Wilder argued, "I've never done anything like that."

Jaylen interrupted him. "Yeah, but your ancestors have. And it's their blood running through your veins right now."

Mr. Wilder raised his index finger before speaking. "Let's make one thing clear. My name is Mr. Wilder. And, as I was saying, I've never done anything like that. Nor do I plan to. In fact, I was hired to teach you how to improve your writing, which means that I am here to help you, Jaylen. Not steal or kill. Now, I can't speak for my ancestors simply because I wasn't alive back then, and I prefer to live in the moment." Jaylen silently looked up at Mr. Wilder with his head tilted to the side.

Mr. Wilder continued. "Now, if you decide not to read it, that's fine too. You both can just sit quietly until it's time for you to leave. And I'll turn my Led Zeppelin back on."

Curtis quickly spoke up. "Jaylen, please read that shit! I'm not trying to hear any more of that wack-ass music."

Jaylen pulled the balled-up paper out of his pocket. "Okay, I'll read it."

Mr. Wilder grinned with excitement. "So who is it for?"

Jaylen was offended. "A girl, obviously! Don't listen to Curtis's dumb ass. I'm *not* gay!"

"Calm down. I know you're not gay. I meant, does she have a name?"

"Oh, her name is Zoe. I've been working on it for a minute. I was going to give it to her tomorrow during lunch."

"Ok. Go ahead."

He coughed to clear his throat before reading.

Zoe, you look more beautiful every day,
I still get butterflies when you walk my way.

You have smooth brown skin and a beautiful smile,

I guess it goes without saying that I'm diggin' your style.

We've been in the same class a handful of times,

I bet you never knew I had a few rhymes.

You're the greatest girl ever, and that's no pretend.

Hey, Zoe, do you want to be my girlfriend?

Jaylen raised his eyebrows, nervously looking up at Mr. Wilder. Mr. Wilder told him he did a good job as he clapped his hands in applause.

Curtis sat at his desk, laughing hysterically. He had to catch his breath to speak. "Oh my God. Jaylen, you are the worst! 'I bet you never knew I had a few rhymes'? She still don't after hearing that shit!" Jaylen balled up his poem and threw it toward the trashcan, but missed. He crossed his arms and thrusted himself into the back of his chair.

Mr. Wilder picked Jaylen's poem up off the floor and placed it on his desk. He looked over at Curtis. "What about this rap of yours? Let's hear what you got."

Curtis stood up with his hand on his chest. "See, Mr. Wilder, the difference between us is that I don't write poems for a girl. I write raps for all the girls. As soon as I start spittin', they just be flockin' toward me."

Mr. Wilder spoke up. "Well, are you going to talk about it for an hour or say it?"

31

Curtis smacked his lips and grabbed a folded-up sheet of paper out of his back pocket. "All right, y'all. Clap your hands like this." Curtis demonstrated. Mr. Wilder and Jaylen grudgingly clapped. Curtis rapped.

"Yeah. Yeah. Check it. Yo, my dick so long that I gotta use the kiddie stall—"

They both stopped clapping immediately. Mr. Wilder threw up both hands to cut him off. "No, no, no, no, no!" Jaylen's entire face was red from intense laughter.

Curtis asked, "What? What's wrong? That's the type of stuff I like to write."

Mr. Wilder replied, "That's fine if that's where your creativity takes you. I would just rather read it than hear it is all." Curtis nodded. Suddenly, all of them turned to watch DeSean walk in and sit in the seat furthest back in the middle row.

2

Even though he already knew the answer, Mr. Wilder wanted to initiate a conversation with the young man. "What's your name?"

DeSean made eye contact with Mr. Wilder to acknowledge that he'd heard him and then dropped his head to pick at his fingernails. His large, puffy afro was pulled back into a thick ponytail held together by a beige rubber band. It stuck straight up in the air, and it was the only thing Mr. Wilder could see from the front of the classroom as the young man continued to sit silently.

Very little time went by before Mr. Wilder questioned Jaylen and Curtis about DeSean. Jaylen reached up with his muscular arm to scratch his small, unkempt afro featuring a fresh lineup. He shrugged his shoulders. "Nah, I don't know his name, white man." Mr. Wilder gritted his teeth and slightly shook his head. He looked back at Jaylen out of the corner of his eye.

Curtis answered, "I don't know him either. I mean, I've seen him around school a few times, but I don't know his name. Based off what I smelled when he walked in, though, I think we should call him Stank Ass."

DeSean quickly stood up with his fists balled. "You better watch your mouth, Curtis!"

Curtis grinned toward Mr. Wilder. "A, yo, Mr. Wilder! You see that? He knows who I am, but I don't know him. I told you I was popular."

Mr. Wilder tried to defuse the situation. "Curtis, be quiet, and turn around in your seat."

While waving him off, Curtis replied, "For what, Mr. Wilder? I ain't worried about him. He needs to sit his ass down before I beat him with a bar of soap." Jaylen burst out laughing. DeSean walked hastily toward Curtis but was cut off by Mr. Wilder. He grabbed DeSean and guided him back to his seat.

Now limping down the aisle back to his desk, Mr. Wilder pointed to Curtis. "I don't want to hear anymore trash talk out of you! There are already two people in this room who want to hurt you. And your mouth isn't helping you out any!"

Jaylen said, "Speaking of help, white man, ain't you supposed to be helping me with my poem? Or are you gonna lie like your ancestors did and break your promise? I mean, if that's the case, that's cool. I'm used to it."

Mr. Wilder went and stood directly in front of Jaylen's desk. "I never made you any promises, Jaylen. I said I was here to help, and I still am. I just haven't had time to get to you yet. So that means I'm not a liar." Mr. Wilder crossed his arms. "Now, please, tell me what promise my ancestors made you that they didn't keep."

Jaylen looked up at Mr. Wilder. He answered with tight lips. "Forty acres and a mule."

Mr. Wilder bent over to put his knuckles on Jaylen's desk. "Jaylen, listen to me very carefully. General Sherman promised forty acres and a mule to former enslaved African American farmers. Yes, you are an African American. But have you ever been enslaved?"

"Nah."

"Have you ever been a farmer?"

"Nah."

"Okay. So my ancestors didn't break their promise to you, because they didn't make a promise to you. Now, if you can find a former-ly enslaved, African American farmer, I would be open to hearing his complaints." Mr. Wilder lowered his voice. He leaned close enough for Jaylen to feel his body heat and the warmth of his breath atop Jaylen's thin mustache. "Until then, you better not call me 'white man' again. Or I will punch you in the mouth so hard that I'll knock your teeth down your throat so that you can have some white in *you*. Are we on the same page?" Jaylen silently nodded to avoid further ridicule from Curtis.

Mr. Wilder retraced his steps to the front of his desk. "By no means am I a history teacher. But to add to what I said, it was you all's ancestors who fought for equality. And that's exactly what we have today—equal-ity. No one in this room was born with forty acres and a mule, including myself. So since we're all born with nothing, we have a choice. We can either look back, complain about the past, and study why we are where we are now, or we can look forward and do something about it. The choice is completely up to you." The three young men briefly looked around at one another silently. The old wooden desk chairs crackled with every motion.

Curtis said, "You're the teacher. Tell us what we should do."

"Well, I believe everyone has a great story to tell. And since this is a creative writing class, that means that the sole purpose of its existence is to help you tell that story. Which, if done correctly, could also make you a lot of money." He glanced over at Jaylen. "Then you can buy yourself forty acres and a mule."

The young men snickered. Mr. Wilder appeared puzzled as Curtis explained, "A, yo, Mr. Wilder. Everybody know that book shit is played out."

Jaylen added, "Yeah, and even if it wasn't, ain't nobody trying to hear what three young black men from the inner city gotta say."

Curtis chimed in. "Unless it's another black man. And I don't know too many of them that like to read."

Jaylen nodded at Curtis's comment. "Look, Mr. Wilder, or whatever your name is. We're all upperclassmen. Me and Curtis are juniors. And I think the dude back there is a senior. So just give us a few creative words we can put on our resumes to get a job." The three young men continued to laugh softly.

Mr. Wilder dropped his head, shook it, and smacked his lips in disappointment. "I can't believe what I'm hearing. As a middle-aged Caucasian, I see young black men like yourselves on the news all the time for some of the craziest things. I say to myself, 'If only they had someone to show them the right way, a different approach, or to just give them a chance. They wouldn't be that way.' I see now, though. I was wrong. You all's problem isn't lack of instruction. You all's problem is yourselves. Why would you all call yourselves black men?"

They looked around at each other, squinting and shrugging their shoulders before Jaylen said, "Um...that's what we see every day in the mirror."

Mr. Wilder put his hand up with his eyes closed. "No. No. No. You still don't understand. Jaylen, you look pretty athletic. Do you play any sports here at Booker T.?"

Jaylen answered, "Not now, but I used to play football my ninth- and tenth-grade years."

"Okay, and by playing that sport and being a student here, what did they call you?"

"A student athlete."

"Exactly! A student athlete. Not an athlete student. Because you being a student is more important and takes precedence over you being an athlete! So why would you call yourself a black man when there's nothing further from the truth? You all are men who just happen to be black. Think about it. When you're facing adversity and a decision has to be made, you don't ask yourself, "What would a black person do in this situation?" No! You say, "What would a man do in this situation?" The fact that you are black should be viewed as an honor and not a hindrance. You all have a heritage of fighters, survivors, and trailblazers. Hell, this whole goddamned country was built by you all's ancestors. I'm not saying that it was right for them to do it, but they did it. Either way, even if I took all your heritage away and painted you blue, green, yellow, or pink, you would still be a man. And until you all begin to see yourselves that way, there will always be a limit to your accomplishments."

The room was so quiet, they could hear the vibration of the motor in the heater beneath the windows. Breaking the silence, DeSean stated his name. "DeSean Briggs."

Curtis reacted with a smile full of perfectly straight, pearly white teeth. "Ohhh! Stank Ass got a name!" DeSean smacked his lips and slightly shook his head. Jaylen giggled.

Mr. Wilder remained calm. "Thank you for sharing that with us, DeSean."

With his forearms relaxed on his desk, DeSean responded, "I like what you said. But it made me think of a question."

Mr. Wilder stuck out his hand and poked out his bottom lip to say, "Go ahead."

DeSean proceeded. "Since you were talking to us about not limiting our accomplishments, I want to know how you're here. You only come in on Tuesdays for two hours after school. And you don't look old enough to be retired."

Mr. Wilder answered with a smile, putting his glossy, coffee-stained teeth on display. "Good observation, DeSean. Technically, I am retired. I retired when I was thirty-two from a chicken plant. I worked as a night-shift supervisor and made extra cash on my time off as a brick mason. Luckily, I made a couple of good investments in the stock market that allowed me to do it."

Jaylen thought, "That explains his large hands and solid physique."

DeSean nodded as Jaylen's lips turned crooked to speak. "Hold up. I saw you pull up in the parking lot in that beat-up old Chevy. That ain't ballin'."

Curtis chimed in. "Yeah, but, Jaylen, a lot of rich people drive regular cars so you don't know who they are. I bet he got a phat-ass crib with a pool on the water, though. And naked hoes serving him bologna sandwiches and Kool-Aid in a wine glass and shit. Right, Mr. Wilder?"

Mr. Wilder swung his head left and right before replying, "Nope. I live in a one-bedroom apartment across the street behind Church's Chicken." The three appeared mystified. Mr. Wilder explained, "You guys shouldn't equate materialistic things with money. I'm a forty-seven-year-old man from the suburbs. I'm not a rapper. You all would be shocked at how many people you think are "ballin'" are actually only one paycheck away from losing it all. Or they have so much debt, they can't even imagine paying it off. My point is, just because you have money doesn't mean that you have to go around buying stupid crap to let others know that you have money. Nothing good comes from that, if you think about it. Besides the fact that you now have less money and presumably more junk, consider the people in your life. If they're not asking for it, they're trying to take it. Or they try to make you feel guilty for having it by calling you names like 'lucky.' Better yet, they'll remind you of a time they did something for you so they can turn around and say, 'You would've never got that money if it wasn't for me.' And if you think that money will afford you new friends, you're right. But you just need to know that as fast as they show up when they find out you have money, they will leave just as fast when they find out that you don't." Mr. Wilder could tell from the blank stares he received that they were giving serious thought to what he'd said.

Curtis couldn't let it rest. "A, yo, Mr. Wilder. So you saying you don't buy nice things for yourself?"

Mr. Wilder rolled his eyes as he exhaled. "What I'm saying, Curtis, is that nice things don't mean shit. What makes the world go around is in your wallet, but it is what's in your mind that will determine what's in your wallet." Mr. Wilder used his fingers to squeeze his bottom lip as he thought briefly before finishing. "Hypothetically speaking, let's say someone came in here right now and said he would pay one million dollars to whomever could write the best novel in this room. Curtis, you're clearly the best dressed in this room and seem to have the nicest things. However, I would be the one to win that money, because I've used my mind to learn a skill. I've used my time to develop that skill. I've put in the work to perfect that skill. So yes, that guy might give you a compliment. But he's going to give me the check."

Curtis dipped his thumbs in his pockets and leaned back in his chair. He looked up at Mr. Wilder with his head tilted.

"With you all being so interested in my personal life, it reminds me that we need to set the tone for this class." After a quick glance at their faces, Mr. Wilder confirmed, "Yes. I said 'we.' This class can be as open or as restricted as you all want it to be. It doesn't make a bit of difference to me."

Jaylen spoke up after shrugging his shoulders while twisting his hair. "Shid, I say everybody just speak they mind." DeSean and Curtis both nodded silently.

"All right." Mr. Wilder said. "What about you all's beloved *N* word?"

Curtis smacked his lips. "A, yo, Mr. Wilder. We really only use that on some respect or friendship type stuff."

DeSean added, "Yeah. But don't you go saying it!"

Mr. Wilder shook his head. "No. No. The rules are the rules in this class. Everyone must abide by them, including myself. So either we all can say the *N* word, or none of us can say the *N* word. But need I remind you that I'm a highly opinionated, middle-aged Caucasian from the rural South? So when I use the *N* word, it won't be friendly."

The three students looked around at each other before saying, all at once, "Fuck no! Hell nah, hell nah. Ain't gonna be no *N* word in here. Nope!"

Mr. Wilder looked down at his watch. The time was now a quarter past five. Knowing that the late bus arrived at five thirty, he pressed on anyway. In a vain attempt to speed up, Mr. Wilder stood up from his desk and smacked his hands together loudly to regain full attention. He rushed his speech. "Okay. Now that that's done, let's get down to business. I'm going to give you all an assignment that is due next Tuesday when we meet." They all griped and moaned about having to do work outside of school. Jaylen took that time to put on his book bag and stand near the classroom door in anticipation of sprinting to the late bus.

Mr. Wilder raised his voice. "Listen! This is not a homework assignment! So don't treat it like one! Or it will suck and be a waste of your time!" The young men regained focus. "I want you all to come up with one good story, and write it down. It doesn't have to be long. Just enough to make it a good story. And when I say a good story, I mean I want it to be so good that if someone would've told it to you, you would've asked them to tell you twice." Jaylen was becoming jittery at the door as Mr. Wilder concluded. "Have a great week. And I'll see you all next Tuesday." Jaylen swung the door open and sprinted out into the hallway.

Mr. Wilder asked, "If either of you need to catch the late bus, then I suggest that you start running now. You don't have much time."

They both stood up. DeSean was moving faster than Curtis. He yanked his large book bag off the floor. "I walk home every day."

Mr. Wilder stared into DeSean's eyes as he walked toward him to exit the classroom. He questioned the validity of DeSean's living situation, but decided not to pester him. He thought, "Whatever he has going on will come up sooner or later."

DeSean sped out of the classroom. Curtis dragged his feet toward Mr. Wilder. "My mama coming to pick me up, if she's not already outside."

Sarcastically, Mr. Wilder commented, "Well, try not to look so happy about it. Come on, I'll walk with you. It's one of my duties to wait with kids who are waiting for their parents to pick them up."

"Oh, they probably making you do that because that's how my boy LaVeon got killed."

"You knew LaVeon Kirkland?"

"Hell yeah! We were boys. He was the only dude in the school more popular than me." Mr. Wilder gripped the hair on the bottom of his goatee as he thought, "I've never heard of a straight-A student being one of the most popular kids at school. That doesn't make any sense."

"A, yo, Mr. Wilder. You okay?"

"Yeah, yeah. I'm fine. Come on, let's get out of here." The two walked out of the classroom. Immediately, Mr. Wilder saw DeSean from the back, walking into the cafeteria down the hallway. Mr. Wilder stopped again to give thought to DeSean's actions.

He couldn't think clearly, though, with Curtis in his ear. "A, yo, watch it Mr. Wilder. You almost scuffed my new tennis shoes!"

Mr. Wilder exhaled. "Sorry about that, Curtis." The two continued to walk.

"It's cool. It's probably just that gout flaring up again in your big toe, huh? The same thing be happening to my uncle Hewitt. What you need to do is drink some 2 percent milk and start running in place. That'll get rid of all of that."

Mr. Wilder rolled his eyes. "Thanks for the tip, Curtis. But I don't have gout. I stopped to think for a second."

Curtis turned his nose up at Mr. Wilder. "You had to stop to think? I don't know how to tell you this, Mr. Wilder, but you would make for a horrible drug dealer."

Mr. Wilder shook his head, hoping that the memory of Curtis's last comment would fall out. "Can you tell me why you don't seem to be in a rush to get home?" Mr. Wilder asked.

"Who wants to rush to the most realistic place in the world? That shit ain't cool. A, yo, I got big dreams! Most people who don't, though, they say I'm 'thinkin' out the box.' And I understand that. But my own dad, though? Really? That dude stay on me with some average guy shit." Curtis began mocking his father's deep voice. "'*You need to be working now so you can build up your resume. You should join the ROTC to help get you some rank like me. Why didn't you apply to those colleges like I asked you?*'" Mr. Wilder nodded as Curtis went on. "Don't get me wrong. I know I'm going to have to work hard at whatever I do. I don't mind doing that. But I feel like if I'm going to work hard at something, then it should be something I want to do, not what other people think I should be doing."

Mr. Wilder looked Curtis in the eye. "I see your point."

"See, and what you just did is more than my father has. He won't even hear me out when I try to explain this to him. A, yo, Mr. Wilder. My role model is Will Smith. He said one time, 'Being realistic is the most commonly traveled road to mediocrity.' I believe that. And that's why you always see me hanging out with Officer Timmons. He encourages me to believe in my dreams. I know we joke each other all the time, but I couldn't imagine not having him here to talk to."

Mr. Wilder wondered aloud, "I understand. So what is it that you want to be?"

Curtis's smile stretched from ear to ear. His eyes were lit with joy. "A comedic rapper." Mr. Wilder tilted his head in confusion. "You know, like Weird Al Yankovic. Except I'm black. And there's nobody black doing it on a high level like that either. I know people would fall out laughing if they heard my stuff. I got mad super-funny raps too." They'd approached the main door when Curtis said, "Oh, and don't be going around telling everybody my business about my dad."

Mr. Wilder reassured him. "Don't worry. I won't."

"Oh, I ain't worried. Cause if you did, I would start clowning yo' ass."

Mr. Wilder smacked his lips. "Curtis, when you get to be forty-seven years old like I am, you don't care much about what people think of you. Especially not some spoiled, snotty-nosed teenage boy." Curtis became straight-faced as Mr. Wilder resumed. "I said I would keep this conversation between us out of respect for your privacy, not fear of your jokes."

Curtis avoided eye contact with Mr. Wilder as he replied, "Okay." He pushed the door slightly. His mother's black BMW X3 was visible through the doors' windows.

"Hold on," Mr. Wilder said abruptly as he leaned down hard on his cane. "I just wanted to tell you that with hard work, dedication, and consistency, I believe you can accomplish your dreams too. You see, one of my role models is Albert Einstein. And he once said, 'Never give up on what you really want to do. The person with big dreams is more powerful than the one with all the facts.'" Curtis nodded as they both walked out into the warm evening breeze.

"A, yo, I like that Mr. Wilder. Thank you." He dipped his head to show acceptance.

After parking her SUV alongside the curb, Curtis's mom got out. She rushed to greet Mr. Wilder with fervor. "You must be Mr. Wilder. It's so nice to meet you, sir."

They shook hands. "It's nice to meet you too, ma'am." The petite woman with frazzled, black hair and caramel, smooth skin apologized. "Oh, I'm sorry. My name is Laura, Laura Jordan. I'm Curtis Jr.'s mother." Curtis rolled his eyes and shook his head. "I just wanted to tell you that I'm so thankful that you're here at the school, and that this knucklehead boy of mine stayed late for your class." Mrs. Jordan plucked Curtis on the side of the head. "I know the stuff he writes is a little goofy, but he loves doing it. And I'm just so happy that he has somebody now who can teach him what to do with all that. You know what I mean?"

While looking her in the eye, Mr. Wilder answered, "Yes, ma'am. I know exactly what you mean. I love creative writing myself. And I think with Curtis's unique twist on things, it will be a great experience for all parties involved."

Mrs. Jordan placed her hand on her chest and exhaled. "I'm so glad to hear that. But I do need to go. It was really nice meeting you, though, Mr. Wilder." She began walking back to the BMW and turned around to wave Curtis on. "Boy, come on! We need to hurry up and get home before your crazy-tail daddy starts blowing my phone up."

As they pulled away, Mr. Wilder thought, "I should rush to the cafeteria and see what DeSean is up to." He turned around swiftly and bumped Jaylen's lips with his shoulder.

"Whoa! Slow down, Mr. Wilder. I almost knocked you down right there." Jaylen said lightheartedly.

Mr. Wilder thought, "Since when did you start calling me Mr. Wilder?" before asking, "Where did you come from? I didn't see you."

"I ran after the bus, but I missed it. So then I ran over here to see if somebody could give me a ride."

Mr. Wilder thought again, "So that's why you're being so polite all of a sudden." He said, instead, "Where are you headed?"

"I need to go to the Burger King on Tidewater Drive."

Mr. Wilder frowned while he thought, before saying, "Okay, I'll take you. Just wait here a minute. I need to run to the cafeteria."

Jaylen shot his arm out to grab Mr. Wilder's wrist. "Sir, I really need to go right now. That's where I work, and my shift starts at six o'clock."

"What?"

"I know I'm doing a lot by rushing you at the last minute like this. But I can hook you up with some food when we get there. And it'll be way better than that cafeteria crap you're about to go get." To keep his agenda of investigating DeSean's suspicious behaviors from Jaylen, Mr. Wilder agreed to take him right away and get food from Burger King.

Standing at the car, Jaylen asked, "Mr. Wilder, why is that old bald-headed janitor staring at us?"

Mr. Wilder looked up and noticed that it was the same janitor from the week before. This time, though, the man with the well-groomed, all-white goatee did not turn away when Mr. Wilder looked back at him.

The two observed each other for a brief moment before Mr. Wilder uttered softly, "I don't know what's wrong with him. But from the way he's gritting his teeth, it seems he's angry about something." Mr. Wilder looked down at his watch. The time was 5:50 p.m. "We need to go if we're going to make it on time."

Jaylen hurried to open the door and noticed the mound of random junk in the passenger seat and back seat. "Where am I supposed to sit?"

Mr. Wilder started the car. "Just throw that crap in the back seat with the rest of it." After doing so, Jaylen saw that the beige, cloth seat had so many coffee stains on it that it looked like desert fatigues. He grimaced in disgust. Jaylen quickly looked around the parking lot one last time for any other option before sitting next to Mr. Wilder.

"I liked your poem." Mr. Wilder said. His compliment grabbed Jaylen's attention and broke the silence in the car. "It was heartfelt and genuine. As a creative writing teacher, there is not much that I can do with that, though, because you're writing for one person. As a man, though, I can tell you that I think she'll like it."

Jaylen looked back at Mr. Wilder with a grin. "Really? You think so?"

"Oh yeah. I always say honesty is the best policy when it comes to matters of the opposite sex."

"Cool. Thanks for the advice, Mr. Wilder."

"Not a problem. So what are your plans with Zoe? What do you hope happens from all of this?"

Jaylen sat up. "Hopefully, one night while my mama at work and my lil' sister sleep, I can sneak her in through my bedroom window. Then, I'ma run to my mama bathroom and grab her baby oil—"

"Whoa! Whoa! Whoa!" Mr. Wilder shouted with his head snapped back.

"What?"

"You need to lie."

"Huh? But what about all that 'honesty is the best policy' stuff you just said?"

"Forget all of that. Your ass needs to lie."

Jaylen smacked his lips and flopped back in his seat.

"So your mother works nights, huh?"

"Yep, and days too. She got two full-time jobs."

"Wow. Now that's a hard-working woman. What about your dad? What does he do?"

Jaylen shrugged his shoulders. "I don't know. He says he's an entrepreneur. But he left my mom about two years ago to be with another woman."

Mr. Wilder glanced over at Jaylen. "I'm sorry to hear that. But what about your little sister?"

"Ain't no need to be sorry, Mr. Wilder. I haven't seen him in a while, but he's still a great dad. We talk all the time." Jaylen turned to look out of the passenger window. "And my lil' sister straight. She be at home with our grandma until I get off."

Mr. Wilder nodded "That's good on you, Jaylen. Getting a job to help your mom out with some of the bills is a really mature thing for someone to do at your age. That's something to be proud of."

Jaylen looked down at his lap and picked at his fingernails. "Thanks. I wish I could take the credit for it, but I can't. I want to play football, but I can't. My dad says that being an entrepreneur doesn't pay well at first. So that's why his child support payments are far and few between. And I had to quit football to get a job."

Mr. Wilder gritted his teeth in anger, thinking, "A kid has to give up his dreams because of a fucking dead-beat dad." All that came out, though, was, "I understand."

"You can pull in right here and park in the back." Mr. Wilder followed his instructions. Jaylen grabbed his work shirt out of his book bag and put it on overtop his white T-shirt. With his work hat in hand, Jaylen looked down at his balled-up fists before getting out. "Oh, and don't think for one second that you can whip my ass either. Cause you can ask anybody around school. These hands is vicious."

Mr. Wilder thought, "Of course you would say that after I've already given you a ride."

"The only reason I let you say that shit to me earlier was because it was a test."

Mr. Wilder wondered aloud, "What do you mean 'it was a test'?"

Jaylen looked up to face him. "It was a test to see if you have balls or if you're afraid of an angry tall black teenage boy calling you white man. I do it to all my white male teachers on their first day. What's crazy is that even though you're handicapped, nobody ever stood up to me quicker than you did."

Mr. Wilder leaned toward Jaylen and gazed into his eyes with a grin. "Vicious or not, a pool table couldn't hold my fucking balls." They shared a hearty laugh.

Mr. Wilder scratched his head. "That's one hell of a way you have to test a man."

"Yeah, I know it's unusual, but it works. The only teacher who didn't stand up to me was Mr. Schmidt. And he shot LaVeon, who was unarmed, in the back. All the other students called him Riley. But I called him white man. And he just went right along with it. He never even looked me in the eye like you're doing right now." There was a brief silence prior to Jaylen saying, "Anyway, I need to get to work. Thanks for the ride, Mr. Wilder." As Jaylen turned to open the passenger door, Mr. Wilder noticed a large keloid scar on the back of Jaylen's head. It caused a natural part in his small afro. Jaylen closed the door behind himself.

"Hey, Jaylen! What happened to the back of your head?"

Jaylen bent over to rest his forearms on the car door and leaned his head into the window. "Remember I told you I quit playing football after my sophomore season to get a job? That wasn't the entire truth. When my dad first left, I tried selling drugs to get the money so I could keep playing ball. When my mom found out, that night when she came home from work, she grabbed a brick from the front yard. Then she came in my room while I was sleep and busted me in the back of the head with it. I just re-member seeing a lot of blood before I blacked out. When I woke up, I was lying in a hospital bed. My mama was right beside me, holding my hand and crying. She told me right then and there that she would kill me herself before she sits back and watches me get killed behind some drugs."

Mr. Wilder raised his eyebrows, pleasantly surprised at Jaylen's sto-ry. "Hell of a woman, your mother is."

Jaylen rubbed the scar. "Don't I know it?" He tapped the car door twice and walked backward toward the restaurant. "Just go through the drive-through, and I'll meet you at the window!"

"What you want?" a woman's voice in the drive-through speaker asked with hostility.

Mr. Wilder was offended. "Is that how you greet all your customers?"

"All the ones who know Jaylen, yes. Now, what you want?"

Mr. Wilder shook his head. "I'll have a whopper with no cheese, medium fries with no salt, and a cup of water with no ice."

"Ew. Sir, you do know that Jaylen taking care of you, right?"

"Yes. And I also know that this is Burger King, where I can have it my way."

"Yeah, but your way nasty, though." The woman read the order aloud for Mr. Wilder to confirm. It was also an opportunity for her cook, pre-sumably one of her girlfriends, to hear. "Anyway, girl, listen to this. He ordered a whopper with no cheese or onions, some flavorless-ass fries with no salt, and a boring cup of water with no ice."

Mr. Wilder could hear the friend respond in the distance, "Ew. Don't he know Jaylen taking care of him? Girl, where they do that at?"

"I don't know. But it sure ain't in Norfolk."

Mr. Wilder corrected the woman. "Excuse me, but I never said no onions. I would like to keep the onions on the sandwich. Thank you."

"Wait a minute, girl. Make that a whopper *with* onions and no cheese."

Her girlfriend couldn't believe it. "What? He wants onions on his whopper?"

"Yes, girl. I know…now, look here, mister, don't be walking up on no women with that ol' stank breath swag you 'bout to have, either." Mr. Wilder rested his head on the steering wheel in frustration. "Gone up there to the window. Jaylen waitin' on you."

He put his car back in drive, then yelled out of the window, "The sandwich comes with onions!"

Jaylen reached out of the window. He handed Mr. Wilder his bag of food and thanked him again for the ride to work.

Before Jaylen could shut the sliding glass, Mr. Wilder grabbed his attention. "Hey!"

Jaylen tilted his head up to say, "What is it?"

"You wouldn't happen to know where DeSean lives, would you?"

Jaylen chuckled. "Shid, nah, Mr. Wilder. I don't mess with that dude like that. Wherever he lives must be close though, 'cause he's always the first one to school and the last one to leave."

3

M r. Wilder arrived at Booker T. Washington High School an hour early at two fifteen the following Tuesday. He decided to have a talk with the head football coach about DeSean and his confounding actions. Even though he knew DeSean wasn't on the football team, he figured there had to be some type of rumor mill going around in the locker room about him.

Mr. Wilder hadn't slept all week. He strenuously tried to put clues together about DeSean. Mr. Wilder appeared sluggish as he dragged his feet across the parking lot toward the school. Pair that with a preexisting limp and a cane, and it looked like a stiff wind could've blown him over.

Fortunately, the hallways were clear, with the students still being in class. Mr. Wilder approached the head coach's office door and began to knock. He noticed the office nameplate that read "Head Football Coach: Jay 'Bucky' Buckner." Through the vertical glass on the door, Mr. Wilder saw a muscular young man walking toward him. His neck was thicker than his head. The dark young man yanked the door open. "Can I help you?"

Mr. Wilder spoke up with uncertainty about what to call him. "Yes. I'm looking for, uh, Coach Bucky."

The young man turned sideways and yelled back into the office, "Hey, coach! It's for you! It's the new writing teacher dude!" With the young man turned, Mr. Wilder was able to see the school-issued portable TV stand just beyond the short hallway leading to the oversized coach's office. It was parked in front of an office desk against the back wall. The TV displayed an amateur football game.

Coach Bucky's voice yelled back, "Tell him come in!"

The young man, who stood a stocky six foot one, looked up at Mr. Wilder. "You heard the man." He let go of the door and walked back into the office to sit in front of the TV. Mr. Wilder caught the door, followed him in, and saw Coach Bucky sitting at another desk that wasn't visible from the office door. Coach Bucky's desk was beneath a large window beside a second door that led directly to the boys' locker room.

He stood up and stuck his hand out. "Coach Bucky. To what do I owe the pleasure, Mister..."

"Wilder. Creative writing teacher." Mr. Wilder grabbed his hand and shook it. Coach Bucky was the energetic type. He was tall and had broad shoulders and a blond buzz cut. He always talked fast and smacked on his chewing gum with his mouth open.

When Coach Bucky saw how Mr. Wilder was looking down at the young man, he gripped the young man's shoulders from behind and apologized. "You'll have to excuse ol' Victor Brown, here. All-State linebackers aren't necessarily known for having the best personalities, if you know what I mean." Mr. Wilder was stone faced as he stared back at Coach Bucky. Coach Bucky forced himself to lightly cough, which only acknowledged the awkward moment.

"Yeah. So we were just watching some film of our Friday opponent. You know, taking advantage of his last-period study hall. Every little bit counts on the football field." Coach Bucky leaned over and nudged Mr. Wilder with his elbow, whispering, "And that's the only way a lot of these kids can afford to go to college, if you know what I mean." Mr. Wilder continued to not budge. Coach Bucky took a step back, stuck his chest out, and rested his hands on his hips. "So what can I do you for, Mr. Wilder?"

He was only able to speak briefly before being interrupted. "Well, like I said, I'm the creative writing teacher. And—"

"Yes, I know—you mentioned that. But I gotta tell you, books aren't too high on our priority list in this room, if you know what I mean."

Victor chimed in. "Thank God."

After a quick thought, Mr. Wilder asked, "Can we step out in the hallway?" Coach Bucky complied.

In the hallway, with the office door closed, Mr. Wilder began to speak. "Listen, I wanted to talk to you about one of the students who walked into my classroom last week. His name is DeSean Briggs." Coach Bucky's eyes got big. He crossed his arms while rubbing his chin and looking down at the floor.

Mr. Wilder noticed his reaction. "I've seen some questionable things about him, and I wanted to know if you know anything. Or have there been any rumors going around the locker room about him?"

Coach Bucky took a deep breath and squeezed his arms together tightly. "Look, I probably shouldn't be telling you this. But what the hell. Toward the end of the last school year, in May, I think it was, I would hear my boys talking about one student in particular by giving him little nicknames. You know how high-school boys tease. They would refer to him as the Bad Breath Bandit or Officer Odor. Then, when the new James Bond movie came out, they would call him, Smelly not Stinky. You know, instead of 'shaken, not stirred'?" Mr. Wilder nodded his head. "Anyway, I think you get my point. They would never call him that to his face, though. At least not on my watch. One day, though, like you, I wanted to find out who this kid was. So I found him and had lunch with him right here in my office. He told me that his parents were struggling with the bills at home. With the water being cut off most of the time, it made it hard to take regular showers, let alone do laundry. I told him he could come through my office and use the boys' shower whenever he needed to. I don't have a way to help him with his laundry, though."

Mr. Wilder nodded with his hands in his pockets. "You have a good heart, Coach Bucky."

"Much obliged."

"What about in the summer time, though?"

Coach Bucky threw his hands up in the air and tilted his head. "I don't know what he did during the summer. The school is shut down then. No one can get in this building."

"I understand. Well, thank you for your help." The two shook hands.

"No problem. I wish I knew more, but that's all I know."

"That's fine. It was plenty." Mr. Wilder turned to walk away before being stopped by Coach Bucky.

"Hey, with a man your size, I'm assuming that leg of yours is an old football injury. Where'd you play ball at? What position?"

Now with some distance between the two, Mr. Wilder turned around. "No. I never stepped foot on a football field, even though my father wanted me to. I preferred to stick with the books." This time it was Coach Bucky who appeared stone faced at Mr. Wilder's answer. Mr. Wilder turned again to walk away.

The bell rang to release the teenagers from school. Mr. Wilder headed to his classroom. After he muddled his way through the crowd, he hurried into his classroom. Mr. Wilder immediately slammed the door shut behind himself. With his back against the door, he looked up. Much to his surprise, Curtis, DeSean, and Jaylen were all there, sitting in their same seats from the week prior. It was obvious that Mr. Wilder was most surprised to see Jaylen. He raised his eyebrows at him. "I wasn't expecting to see you again."

Jaylen responded, "Well, this is a creative writing class. So I'm gonna need some help with those lies you recommended." The two chuckled as Curtis and DeSean looked on in confusion.

Mr. Wilder spoke while limping toward his desk. "So let's get to it! Last class I gave you all a homework assignment to *take your time* and come up with a good story. Who'd like to share his first?" Mr. Wilder placed one leg on the edge of his desk and rested his elbow on his lap.

DeSean spoke up. "I'll share."

Mr. Wilder's head popped up in shock. He stuck out his palm. "Please. Go ahead."

"All right. It's a story about a homeless young man who's trying to become a journalist like his deceased father was. Essentially, it's telling how he goes about doing it with no relationship with his mother." DeSean leaned back in his chair and shrugged his shoulders carelessly.

Mr. Wilder thought, "This might be the real story of what he has going on. But why would he offer to go first and expose himself to everyone? And his tone and body language was so nonchalant. It was like he had no emotional attachment to the story at all." Either way, Mr. Wilder gave positive feedback. "I like it. I have questions, but that's a good thing. If someone gives you a summary of a story, and you don't have questions, you can bet it's a bad story. Everyone likes a good journey story. The more hurdles your protagonist has to overcome, the better. I'm assuming it's a drama. Correct?"

Still appearing uninterested, DeSean gave Mr. Wilder a head nod.

"All right. Who's next?" Mr. Wilder asked.

Curtis answered, "A, yo, Mr. Wilder. I don't have the full story all the way laid out yet. But I can tell you what it's about."

"Go ahead."

"Okay. So it's about this middle-aged dude who's been a stripper for a minute. One day, he's influenced by this younger stripper to become a Christian rapper. It's really about the struggles he has trying to break into the rap game. I know it might sound crazy. But it's a good story, and funny too." Mr. Wilder had his head down with a smile on his face. He scratched his eyebrows while thinking.

DeSean reminded Mr. Wilder, "Didn't you say if you have a lot of questions, that makes it a good story?"

Jaylen jumped in. "Shid, if that's the case, Curtis, you got a *New York Times* bestseller."

Curtis responded, "Oh, I know you ain't sitting over there trying to joke with that lil' nappy-ass afro you got. Every time you pick it, it sounds like a kung fu movie. *Ting! Pow! Kung! Bing!*"

Mr. Wilder broke up the chatter. "All right. All right. That's enough. That's enough. Jaylen, sit down." Jaylen slowly took his seat.

"Curtis has a very unique thought process and way of seeing things. The last thing I would want to do is put guidelines on his creativity." He reached up to point toward DeSean and then Jaylen. "Had it been either one of you telling me that story, I would say that you need to try again. But, Curtis, quite frankly, I'm excited to see what you will do with that storyline." Mr. Wilder chuckled. "Least of all, it will make for one hell of a comedy." Curtis slapped his paper down on the desk. He had a smile that could only be contained by the cheeks that surrounded it.

Jaylen sat up in his chair, showing an enthusiastic grin. "To hell with all that. I got an action-packed flick for you, Mr. Wilder."

Curtis chimed in. "Man, ain't nobody trying to read a porno."

Jaylen smacked his lips. "Not a flick like a porno, dumbass. I mean a flick like a story that could be a movie."

"I know. I was just messing with you, Jaylen," Curtis said while still smiling.

Mr. Wilder got things back on track. "Okay, let him talk. Go ahead, Jaylen. I'm anxious to hear."

Jaylen used plenty of hand gestures to explain. "All right, so check this out, right. So you got this father and son, and they're both Green Berets, right. And they just got sent over to China to work together for the first time. China built these big-ass walls to section themselves off from the rest of the world. But here's the cold part, though. If you try to get in, or even fly over, China, they'll shoot your punk-ass down, just like that." Jaylen snapped his fingers. "I'm talkin' about some straight up gangsta shit. So the father and son gotta quietly camouflage themselves and sneak in at night to find out what the big secret is that China's hiding."

Mr. Wilder could tell that Jaylen thought highly of his dad from his story. He told it with great passion. Mr. Wilder nodded. "Yeah. That sounds action packed. I can picture the blood and violence already."

Jaylen added, "The cool part is that the dad is a great shooter. He has the experience to find great hiding places, and he knows how to work silently. The son is great in hand-to-hand combat. He's fast and energetic. Together, they're like the perfect person. Plus, they communicate well because they're family."

Mr. Wilder pursed his lips and looked at Jaylen with big eyes. He was pleasantly surprised by his storyline. "I really liked your story a lot. I love a good shoot-'em-up movie. But what makes your story interesting is that you managed to sprinkle in a little bit of drama with the relationship being between a father and a son. It doesn't take away from the action. It just adds enough sentiment to make your story appeal to a larger audience." Mr. Wilder clapped three times. "I'm very impressed. That's a great story line coming from a first-time writer." Jaylen leaned back in his chair with a closed-mouth grin. His arms were crossed as he nodded back to Mr. Wilder.

Mr. Wilder turned around to grab a fresh piece of chalk out of the box. He wrote on the blackboard, "<u>OUTLINE</u>" as he began to lecture. "First off, let me say that I'm glad you all decided to take your homework assignment seriously. And now that you have a story that you want to tell, the first thing you need to do is outline it." The teenage boys smacked their lips and slouched down in their seats.

Mr. Wilder put his hand up. "Now, wait a minute! I know there isn't a person alive who likes to outline. But it is necessary. There's nothing worse than reading a book where the author is rambling on about meaningless things. It just chaps my ass."

Curtis spoke up. "Um. You might need to go to the free clinic for that, Mr. Wilder." Jaylen and DeSean cackled.

Mr. Wilder shook his head in frustration before he explained to Curtis, "It's just a figure of speech. Another way of saying that it angers me."

Curtis lifted his chin. "Ohh. Okay."

Mr. Wilder continued. "As I was saying, there are many different ways to outline a story. If you compare two of the greatest writers of our time, Stephen King and John Irving, you'll find that they out-line their books completely different. John Irving writes the last sen-tence down first. Then, he has a sequence of events that get him there. Stephen King, on the other hand, will think of a story, start writing it, and sometimes never jot a note down. He'll just go wherever the story takes him." DeSean took notes intensely. Curtis's head lay on his desk while Jaylen barbarously yawned.

"Am I boring you two?" Mr. Wilder questioned.

Jaylen replied, "Hell yeah! We don't know them nig—" Jaylen caught himself as Mr. Wilder's eyes expanded. "We don't know them dudes. The only people we know who be writing shit is Tyler Perry and David E. Talbert."

Mr. Wilder grunted. "Em. Well, let me tell you, there are a lot of other great writers out there. But my point is that whether it's on pa-per or mental, it works for them. So rather than beat you over the head with the traditional formatting of an outline, I will tell you what an outline should do. Then, you can go off and format it however you see fit. And here it is in one sentence: The purpose of an outline is to serve as a reminder of events that take place to make up your story. Period. End of discussion." After they saw how serious Mr. Wilder was during his statement, they all rushed to jot down his last sentence.

Curtis slapped his pen down on his wooden desk. "A, yo, hold up though, Mr. Wilder. What you telling us all this stuff for? We ain't no authors. We just tryin' to tighten up our lil' raps and poems." Jaylen nodded in agreement with Curtis.

Mr. Wilder stood in front of his desk. He leaned on his cane with one hand while the other was in his pocket. He looked up at his three students and exhaled softly. "Because you all are going to write a novel."

As Mr. Wilder expected, Jaylen and Curtis nagged and complained. They even gathered their things and began to walk out of the classroom. "Man, you *got* to be fuckin' trippin'. You must be smoking that good shit," Jaylen said.

Curtis followed. "Hell yeah. Ain't nobody got time to be writing that long-ass shit."

Mr. Wilder mentioned, with a calm tone, "You could win $20,000."

Jaylen, who stood in front of Curtis at the door, turned his head to learn more. "What you mean? Like a competition?"

Before Mr. Wilder could answer, Curtis interrupted him. "Obviously," followed by him tapping Jaylen on the shoulder. "Come on, Jay. Let's go. Don't listen to that man. We ain't got no chance in hell of winning that money. Think about it. With that kind of money on the line, you know motherfuckas who write all the time gonna be in that shit." Jaylen agreed.

They were about to exit the room when Mr. Wilder said, "Yes. You're right, Curtis. But those 'motherfuckas' can't write about something they've never done better than some 'motherfuckas' who've done it. Like you said, Curtis, 'Think about it.' Who can write a funnier story than a 'motherfucka' who jokes people all day? And, Jaylen, who can write a more violent story than a 'motherfucka' who likes to fight?"

There was a moment of tense silence before Mr. Wilder, Jaylen, and Curtis looked back at DeSean. He was still sitting in his seat with a grin on his face. "What? I like to write."

Jaylen and Curtis briefly looked at each other, then turned around to take their seats.

"A, yo, Mr. Wilder. Tell us some more about this competition," Curtis requested.

With both hands now in his pockets and his cane resting against his desk, Mr. Wilder paced the floor in front of his desk. "Okay. It's an annual novelist competition held right here in Norfolk at The Scope. It's called the Grand Writer Awards. It's hosted by Summit's Creek Publishing House. It takes place in early December."

Jaylen smacked his lips. "Man, get to the part about the money."

"So there are four winners every year—two in each age group, the age groups being high schoolers and adults. For the high schoolers, which would be you two," Mr. Wilder said, pointing at Curtis and Jaylen, "you can win a $20,000 publishing contract for your novel from Summit's Creek Publishing House and a $40,000 scholarship to any college of your choice. There will be one winner for best fiction and one winner for best nonfiction. None of that second place, everyone's a winner bullshit." From the way that Curtis and Jaylen continued to nod at one another, it seemed to Mr. Wilder that they were up for the challenge.

Mr. Wilder stopped pacing the floor. He squared his shoulders and faced the students. "Now, for you, DeSean, since you're already eighteen, you'll be competing in the adult group. It's the same categories but a different prize. The winners in your group will get a $60,000 contract. But obviously, there will be no scholarship because they're all adults. How does that sound to you, Mr. Briggs?"

DeSean stood abruptly. He held his stomach and said, with a break in his voice, "That sounds real good, Mr. Wilder. Real good. But I gotta run to the bathroom real quick. I'll be back."

While DeSean gathered his things to leave, Curtis asked, "That's enough money to make you shit yourself, huh, DeSean?" Even though Curtis was able to get a reaction out of Jaylen, DeSean and Mr. Wilder ignored him. DeSean threw his book bag over his shoulder and began to walk out of the classroom.

Mr. Wilder thought aloud, "Why are you taking all of your things with you?"

DeSean didn't stop walking. He shrugged his shoulders. "I don't know y'all like that." DeSean hurried out of the classroom.

Mr. Wilder checked his watch. The time was 5:10 p.m. Mr. Wilder didn't believe DeSean had to use the restroom, and he wanted to chase after him. He couldn't, though. He was obligated to five more minutes in the classroom. However, still anxious and curious, Mr. Wilder tapped his fingers rhythmically on his desk as he leaned against it. He thought, "I can just release the other two so I can find out what DeSean is up to."

Mr. Wilder rushed to address them. "Okay, Jaylen and Curtis. I want to see your outlines next week when we meet. I'll see you then. Have a good week." Mr. Wilder took one fast step toward the door but was stopped by Jaylen.

"Hold up, Mr. Wilder. How do you outline your books?" Curtis nodded silently in agreement. Both students clenched their pens, prepared to write everything that Mr. Wilder was about to say.

Mr. Wilder thought, "It figures that Jaylen would be the one to ask me a question right now. He hardly ever speaks in here. Either way, I'm going to hurry up and answer this question so that I can still try to catch DeSean."

He explained, "I like to break the story into chapters. Then, in each chapter, I'll write five to eight key things that need to happen. The fun part about writing, to me, is connecting the dots." Mr. Wilder took a couple more steps toward the door before being stopped again.

This time it was Curtis. "A, yo, Mr. Wilder. Can you show us, like, an example or something?" Mr. Wilder felt defeated. He dropped his head, along with any hopes he had of following DeSean, as he limped toward the blackboard.

After Mr. Wilder took the time to draw it all out for them on the blackboard in greater detail, the time was five thirty. Curtis threw his book bag across his shoulders. "You know Stank Ass ain't coming back, don't you?"

Mr. Wilder exhaled. "I figured as much."

Jaylen asked Mr. Wilder for a ride again. He complied. The three left the room together and walked outside.

Curtis's mother patiently waited as she read a novel. When she saw the group, Mrs. Jordan got out of the vehicle. She walked to the passenger side, greeting Jaylen and Mr. Wilder along the way with a smile. Curtis sat in the driver's seat.

Mr. Wilder asked, "What are you reading, Mrs. Jordan?"

"Oh. My book club picked it for this month with Thanksgiving coming up and all. It's a comedic novel called *Thankful for My Family*. It's really funny. I was in the car cracking up before y'all walked out. I heard it's the first of a trilogy. I'ma have to go get the other books too, 'cause this author is a fool."

"Yeah, well, judging from the cover, it looks like it's a hoot."

Jaylen added, "Yeah, I was about to say the same thing."

Mr. Wilder asked, "So you're part of a book club, huh?"

She shamefully laughed. "Yes, I am. You know us stay-at-home mothers have to find something to do. Church gossip gets old after a while."

Mr. Wilder smiled. "Oh, no. I understand...so Curtis is driving now?"

"Yeah. He has his learner's permit now. So my husband and I try to let him drive as often as possible. My husband is still on the fence about buying him a car, though. If you ask him, Curtis Jr. got the attention span of a goldfish." At the last moment, Mrs. Jordan tugged at her seat belt to ensure that it was on as Curtis drove away.

Jaylen had an optimistic, jittery vibe about him that evening that did not go unnoticed by Mr. Wilder. He didn't even hesitate to hop right into the filthy passenger seat of the car.

As Mr. Wilder pulled out of the school's parking lot, he looked over at Jaylen. "Um, is there anything that you want to talk to me about?"

"Who, me? Oh, nah. I'm straight. Thanks for asking, though."

"Oh, sure. No problem. I'll just turn on this Johnny Cash CD I was listening to this morning."

"No! Okay. My dad is coming to get me in a few days so that we can hang out."

Mr. Wilder thought, "It works every time." He responded, "That's great news, Jaylen, and a good reason to be excited."

Jaylen bashfully smiled. "Yeah, he's a super cool dude. I can't wait to see him."

"I bet you can't. So will he be picking you up at school or at home?"

"Oh. At school for sure. My mom and dad can't spend more than five minutes in the same room together. She claims he's not a real man. He says that my mom is just old fashioned."

"Old fashioned in what regard?"

"Well, my mom believes that if you're going to be man enough to impregnate a woman, then you should be man enough to marry that woman and raise your child the right way. When he was living with us, that was an ongoing argument. My mom wasn't going to give him the benefits of being a husband without being married. He called her old fashioned for that."

Mr. Wilder chuckled. "Yeah, well, any pastor will tell you that sex is supposed to be for married people."

"What? I'm not talking about sex! I'm talking about my last name. My mom says that being able to carry on your last name is one of the perks of being a husband, not some random guy with no commitment. She refused to let him have the perks of a husband without the responsibility of one."

"I see her point. So you have your mother's last name?"

"Yep. Jaylen Edwards."

"Wait a minute. Didn't you say that you had a younger sister?"

"Yeah. Same dad, and her last name is Edwards too. It pisses my dad off to no end. So I don't ever talk about it when we're hanging out."

"Yeah, good idea."

Mr. Wilder turned into the Burger King parking lot. Jaylen popped up and put his hands on the dashboard. "Whoa! Whoa! Whoa! Mr. Wilder! My bad. I forgot to tell you I don't have to work today. I just need a ride home. I live on the other side of Tidewater Dr." Jaylen pointed. "Over there, in the Calvert Square Apartments."

Mr. Wilder rolled his eyes and sucked his teeth. Then, he headed that way.

"Sorry about that, Mr. Wilder."

"No problem."

"Hey, remember last week you was telling me that I should lie to Zoe? Like, what type of lies should I say?"

"Huh? Who is Zoe?"

"Remember? The girl I'm trying to get with."

"Oh, yes. No, no, no. Didn't you say you would be hanging out with your father in a few days?"

"Yeah."

"I would wait to ask him. He obviously knows how to say something right if your mother gave him any time of day."

Jaylen nodded. "Yeah that's a good idea, Mr. Wilder. I think I'll do that."

Mr. Wilder glanced over at Jaylen. Then he swiped his hand in a cutting motion, firmly across his throat. "Now, don't you say *anything* to her before that time."

Jaylen pulled his head back. "Um. Okay. Don't worry. I won't. Slow down a little. My apartment is coming up. That's my mom standing on the porch with a cigarette in her mouth."

Mr. Wilder's inability to parallel park was on vivid display. He held up traffic in the far-right lane of Tidewater Drive. Finally, the car was parked. The two made their way to the sidewalk.

They were approached by Jaylen's mother, a thin, fast-talking, confident woman who had her long, natural hair up in a tight ponytail. "Who is he?"

"That's the writing teacher I was talking to you about, mama." The cars zoomed past on the road behind them. They softened everyone's tones.

Mr. Wilder reached out his hand. "Brett Wilder, ma'am. How are you?"

She looked at Mr. Wilder's hand, struck a match, and dipped her head to light the cigarette. She used her hand as a wall to block the wind. As she tossed the match, Mr. Wilder retrieved his hand and straightened his smile.

"Nice to meet you, white man. Tonya Edwards."

"Well, I see the apple doesn't fall too far from the tree, does it?" Jaylen shrugged his shoulders.

"Why y'all getting here so late? Is this going to be a normal thing? Did he tell you that I have to work my second job tonight?"

"Um, I would like to apologize for being late. I take full responsibility for that. My class ran a little long this evening. Secondly, him being late will not be a normal thing. But if you're referring to me giving him a lift afterward, I have no issues with making that a normal thing."

"Good."

"And, no, I wasn't informed of your work schedule."

Ms. Edwards cut her eyes at her son. "Yeah, I bet you weren't."

"But ma—"

"Boy, shut up!" Ms. Edwards checked the time on her watch. "You're the reason I'm running late now!"

Jaylen smacked his lips and his mother went ballistic. "Boy, listen to me! I don't care how many muscles you got! I'm the captain of this shit! Do you understand me?"

"Yes, ma'am."

Mr. Wilder interrupted her. "Um. Excuse me, Ms. Edwards. But I think you meant 'ship.' You're the captain of this ship."

"What? You can hop back in your filthy car and leave this *shit*, Mr. White Man!"

Mr. Wilder threw both his hands up in the air. He slowly began to walk back to the driver-side door.

Ms. Edwards finished talking to Jaylen. "Now, we got a couple cans of ravioli left in there. You can cook that for you and your sister."

"Yes, ma'am." Jaylen started to walk inside the apartment. His mother yelled behind him. "And this house better be clean when I come home too! I spend all day wiping people's asses at the nursing home, and all night mopping floors in office buildings! You think I want to come home and clean up y'all shit too?" The door closed behind Jaylen. Mr. Wilder's car started.

"Hey! Hey! Hey! Wait a minute!" Ms. Edwards knocked on the passenger door window. Mr. Wilder rolled it down. "Hey. All this stuff don't cost nothing, do it? Cause I don't have money for no new bills right now."

"No, ma'am. The creative writing program is completely free."

"Good. So you really think my son got a chance with this writing stuff? I can barely ever get more than two or three words out of him."

"That's good. The quiet ones always have the best stories, because they listen the most. And, yes, I do believe your son has a chance at being a writer. He could make a lot of money at it too, if he's willing to put in the work."

"Well, if it's free, keeps him off the streets and at home most of the time, gives him a chance to make a lot of money, and requires him to work hard, then I like it. I'll support that." Ms. Edwards extended her hand. "Thank you, Mr. Wilder."

Mr. Wilder grabbed her hand, shook it, and looked her in the eyes. "My pleasure."

4

The very next day at six o'clock, among the morning dew, Mr. Wilder's Chevy Lumina creeped into the empty teachers' parking lot. He had no music playing. The sun hadn't risen yet. The streets were so clear that the traffic lights blinked yellow. Mr. Wilder walked to the main entry door and wiped the crust from his eyes along the way. The door was locked. He limped around and checked every entry door to the high school. They were all locked. The sound of the chains rattled with each tug of the doors. To Mr. Wilder, that rattle seemed ten times louder at this time of morning.

Finally, after circling the building, Mr. Wilder arrived at the athletics entry door at a quarter past six. As he anticipated, it was unlocked. He walked through the coach's office to the boys' locker room. The unpleasant smell of sweaty flesh was overwhelming. As Mr. Wilder assumed, DeSean was there. He was in the showers washing himself with a bar of soap while quoting rap lyrics. Mr. Wilder turned his head to look away.

"Hey." The bass in Mr. Wilder's voice echoed throughout the community shower and startled DeSean.

DeSean smacked his lips. "I'm not surprised to see you here." He looked Mr. Wilder up, down, and back up again before turning his back toward him. "I heard you asked the principal and Coach Bucky about me. He couldn't keep a secret if he locked it up and threw away the key."

"Why'd you leave my classroom?"

"I told you, I had to use the bathroom. So I went and took a shit. By the time I came back to class, y'all were already gone. Look, Mr. Wilder, don't worry about me. My outline is already finished."

The steam from the showers sunk into Mr. Wilder's blazer. He silently nodded while looking around and then noticed DeSean's large book bag open on the bench next to him. In his bag were unclean spare clothes with a toothbrush sitting on top. Mr. Wilder knew DeSean had lied to him about using the bathroom. But he wanted DeSean to feel comfortable enough with him to tell the truth. So Mr. Wilder decided to switch to a lighter subject. He figured that would get DeSean talking and make him less hostile.

"So what was that you were singing earlier when I walked in?"

"I wasn't singing. I was rapping…but that was my favorite rap song. 'Hi Life,' by UGK. It's old, so you might've heard it before. Especially being from the south like you say you are."

Mr. Wilder shrugged his shoulders and shook his head. "No, I can't say that I'm familiar with it. What does UGK stand for, maybe?"

DeSean stretched out his hand to plead with Mr. Wilder in a vain attempt to jog his memory. "Underground Kings! You know, Pimp-C… Bun-B? Come on, Mr. Wilder. The *Ridin' Dirty* album? That was a classic."

Mr. Wilder continued to shake his head slowly. "Nope. Sorry, I've got nothing. It doesn't ring any bells."

DeSean smacked his lips. "Yeah, I shouldn't have expected you to know anyway. You wearing a suit on your day off."

Mr. Wilder looked down at his clothing and began to chuckle. "Yeah. I guess you could say I don't have much of a wardrobe." DeSean heard him laughing and joined in.

The amusement came to a subtle end. DeSean's back was still turned to Mr. Wilder. He dropped his arms to his sides, exasperated. "Why are you here? What do you want?"

Mr. Wilder lifted his cane off the floor. He leaned against the bur-gundy-and-white-tiled shower walls. "I want to know your deal. What's your story?"

"Really? I'm surprised Coach Bucky didn't tell you. My dad going through some rough times right now trying to find another job. They keep cutting his hours. Until he does, our water is going to be off for a while."

"You can't bullshit a bullshitter, DeSean. If your water was out at home, you'd still be able to store your clothes there. You must have, like, four or five outfits in that book bag."

"Since our water is out, I use the football laundry room to wash my clothes."

"So you do laundry every day at school?"

"No, not every day."

Mr. Wilder argued, "Yes. It would have to be every day! Because that book bag is filled to the brim every day."

Over the sound of the shower water hitting the floor, Mr. Wilder heard DeSean smack his lips as he clenched his fists. Abruptly, DeSean turned around to face Mr. Wilder. Covered only by soap suds, he exposed himself. With crooked lips, he shrugged his shoulders nonchalantly. "Look. I'm homeless, all right? You happy now?"

Mr. Wilder didn't flinch a muscle. He turned to look back into DeSean's eyes. "Truthfully, I'm not surprised. That's what I thought. But I just needed confirmation. Now that I know, I would like for you to come live with me. I have a couch and—"

"Whoa! Wait a minute. I'm not some charity case. I'm doing okay by myself."

Without warning, the shower door swung open.

"What the fuck is going on in here?" Coach Bucky demanded at first glance of Mr. Wilder watching DeSean shower. DeSean turned back around to rinse off.

Mr. Wilder ignored Coach Bucky's question and continued to speak to DeSean. "DeSean, if you tell me no, I'm telling ol' Coach Bucky here the truth. And you and I both know what that means."

Coach Bucky's eyebrows knitted together in confusion. He backed up while smacking on his chewing gum. "Fuck that! I'm calling security for this shit." Coach Bucky peeked his head into the showers. "You okay in there, DeSean?"

"Yes, Coach, I'm fine."

Coach Bucky was sure not to take his eyes off Mr. Wilder. He raised his voice toward DeSean. "Okay, good! I'll be right back! I'm stepping out to call security!" Coach Bucky pointed. "And as for you, Mr. Wilder, I suggest you start looking for another job."

Coach Bucky ran into his office. Mr. Wilder looked down at his watch. The time was nearing seven o'clock, which meant that school would be starting in thirty minutes, and all staff should've already arrived. At that moment, Mr. Wilder realized Coach Bucky wasn't just blowing smoke up his ass about contacting security. Nonetheless, he remained consistent with DeSean.

"So what will it be?"

DeSean grabbed his towel off the hook and began to dry off. "It don't really seem like I have a choice. I don't want everybody in the school to know. So I guess I have to stay with you…excuse me." DeSean reached for his bag to get dressed.

Coach Bucky burst through the shower door, pointing. "There he is right there, Officer Timmons! I saw him watching DeSean in the shower."

Officer Timmons rushed in directly behind him. His hand rested on his gun holster. Officer Timmons stared at Mr. Wilder as he stood next to DeSean, who was only covered from the waist down in a bath towel. He drew his weapon and aimed it at Mr. Wilder. "Turn around, and put your hands above your head right now!"

With his cane in hand, Mr. Wilder took two steps back and surrendered his hands in the air. "Whoa, Officer Timmons! Calm down now."

"I said hands on your head right now, motherfucker!"

Mr. Wilder complied. "Okay. Okay."

Officer Timmons asked DeSean, "You okay, boy?"

"Yes, sir, I'm fine. But—"

"Shut up, and get dressed! Then meet me down at the principal's office. You can tell your story to her." Officer Timmons approached Mr. Wilder from the rear. He apprehended him and put him in handcuffs. Officer Timmons then returned his gun to its holster, snatched Mr. Wilder by his collar, and shoved him through the locker-room door, which was held open by Coach Bucky.

Coach Bucky complemented Officer Timmons. "That's damn fine police work, Officer."

"Thank you. And thank you for notifying me."

"Absolutely. Anytime, sir. Here, let me get that for you." Coach Bucky opened his office door leading out to the hallway, allowing the two to exit. Officer Timmons continued to use the back of Mr. Wilder's collar to forcefully guide him out into the hallway.

Once they were out in the hallway, Officer Timmons grabbed Mr. Wilder's right elbow with his left hand. He briskly walked alongside him down the long hallway, headed to the principal's office. The hallways were still empty. Most of the early students were in the cafeteria eating breakfast. Mr. Wilder had difficulty keeping up without his cane. He'd been forced to leave it on the boys' locker room floor.

Fueled by anger, Officer Timmons began mocking what Mr. Wilder said in their last conversation. "'Oh. I'm not one of those crazy white boys, Officer Timmons. You don't have to worry about me, Officer

Timmons'…your perverted ass hasn't even been here for a month, and—"

Mr. Wilder yanked his arm away from Officer Timmons. "Hey! I'm not a fucking pervert!"

Officer Timmons quickly drew his weapon. He pressed the barrel of the gun against Mr. Wilder's forehead until his back was against the wall. "Don't you ever snatch your goddamn arm away from me again! I'll put a bullet through your head with a smile on my face, mother-fucker! I don't have no sympathy for y'all pedophiliac perverts! And if I could get rid of just one of y'all, I'd feel like I made the world a better place."

Mr. Wilder was afraid to flinch. Officer Timmons's finger rested on the trigger as the tip of the barrel dug into his skull.

Mr. Wilder whispered, "I'm *not* a pervert, sir."

"Oh yeah? Well, what do you call it when you see a grown-ass man alone with a naked teenage boy in the showers?" Mr. Wilder tried to look Officer Timmons in the eye, but he would've had better luck look-ing in a kaleidoscope.

Vaguely, the two heard the creaking sound of a door opening. Officer Timmons put away his gun as they both looked around curi-ously. It was DeSean, who'd walked out of Coach Bucky's office holding Mr. Wilder's cane.

Mr. Wilder, whose eyes were pierced with rage, started answering Officer Timmons's question as DeSean approached. "Listen to me! I'm not a fucking pervert, pedophile, or any of that other bullshit! I noticed suspicious activity with that boy!" Mr. Wilder used his shoulder to point at DeSean. "And when I asked Principal Akers about him, she ignored me. I could never catch him after class. But Coach Bucky told me where I could find him. And my suspicion was right."

Officer Timmons looked back at Mr. Wilder. His head was tilted with his thumbs dipped in his service belt. "Oh yeah? And what suspicion might that be?"

Mr. Wilder glanced over at DeSean. "I'm sorry, DeSean. But my hands are tied. Officer Timmons, the boy's homeless. And it seems like I'm the only person around here who noticed or even seems to give a damn."

Officer Timmons laughed out loud. "Get the fuck outta here! That boy ain't homeless! That's a damn shame. You'll lie on a kid just to keep your job. Bring yo' ass down here to the principal's office." Officer Timmons grabbed Mr. Wilder's elbow. Mr. Wilder yanked his arm away again. Officer Timmons placed his hand on his gun.

"What! Fuck this job! And fuck you for thinking I would do some shit like that! DeSean, please speak up!"

Officer Timmons asked, "Boy, is this white man telling me the truth?"

DeSean hung his head. "Yeah. Everything he said is true. He even offered me a place to stay at his spot. But please don't tell anybody, though. If this starts spreading around school, I'm not coming back."

Officer Timmons dipped his head in agreement. He took a step back while keeping his eyes on DeSean. "Well, I'll be damned. What about your parents?"

Mr. Wilder added, "Yeah. Good question."

"I don't really want to get into it. But you might as well say they're dead."

"I can understand that," Mr. Wilder said.

Officer Timmons spoke up. "Oh, here. Let me take these handcuffs off you, Mr. Wilder. I'm sorry about all that."

"No. It's okay. After thinking about it, if I were you, I would've done the same thing." Mr. Wilder and Officer Timmons shook hands. DeSean handed Mr. Wilder his cane.

Officer Timmons said, "That's a good thing you're doing, Mr. Wilder. You know, letting the boy stay with you and all. DeSean, you know I would've told you that you could stay at my house too. But me and my wife like to walk around naked. And as bad as my eyesight's been lately, I'm liable to handcuff *yo'* ass to bed."

DeSean blurted out, "Oh hell nah! I'm good at Mr. Wilder's." DeSean took that time to look down at Mr. Wilder's left hand. He noticed that he wasn't wearing a wedding band.

Officer Timmons said, "Well, we still need to go down to the principal's office to make sure that what y'all are doing is okay. You all right with that, DeSean?"

"Yes, sir, I'm fine with that."

At the main office, the three of them walked past the front desk without asking any questions. They barged into the principal's office, closing the door behind themselves. Their actions caused a lot of awkward looks and lip smacks from the vice principal and other female assistants in the front office. Mr. Wilder immediately sat down when he entered. Bothered by the recent long amount of time spent standing, Mr. Wilder began to rub the leg that caused his distinctive limp.

Principle Akers was outraged. She stood and pointed. "You stand up right now, Mr. Wilder! I did not give *you*, of all people, the right to sit in my office!"

Mr. Wilder rolled his eyes and reached for his cane. Officer Timmons stood facing Principal Akers alongside her desk. He put his right hand in the air.

"Everybody, calm down. Calm down. Principle Akers, have a seat. Mr. Wilder, you can stay seated." Principal Akers slowly sat in her seat. She glanced over at DeSean, who stood with his back to her door.

Officer Timmons continued. "Um, Principal Akers, I found out some new information that you might want to hear. Matter of fact, based off what I'm about to tell you, I think that we should be keeping Mr. Wilder around."

"Well, what is it, Timmons?"

"Ms. Akers, the boy is homeless."

She stretched out her neck with her eyes opened wide. "Okay. I knew that already, Timmons."

Officer Timmons lost his cool. "What the fuck you mean you already knew that? Why you ain't say nothing? Or do something about it?"

Principal Akers's face turned red with fear as she leaned back in her chair.

Before she had a chance to answer, Officer Timmons peeked over at DeSean and Mr. Wilder. "And why the fuck are y'all over there looking all calm? Can you believe this?"

DeSean spoke up. "Well, yeah. I can believe it because I told her."

"You told her? Why you ain't tell me you told her?"

DeSean shrugged his shoulders. "You didn't ask."

Officer Timmons shook his head and grabbed something off Principal Akers's desk. "How about I ask you if you want me to throw this coffee on you?"

DeSean put his index finger in the air. "Well, my answer would be no for two reasons. First of all, I'm sure that that would be considered a crime. And, secondly, that's a candle, not a cup of coffee."

Officer Timmons put it back on the desk. "It don't matter. All this shit look the same to me."

Mr. Wilder, as he rubbed his goatee, added, "Listen, I figured she knew from the way she responded to me when I asked about him."

Principal Akers sat up in her chair and stuck her chest out with pride. "Yes, I knew! And I was doing something about it! I gave him whatever money I could afford to give at the end of each week for helping me around the office."

Officer Timmons mumbled, "What type of slavery agreement y'all done worked out around here? No set pay, just set to work. You lucky this ain't Black History Month. I need to teach your ass a lesson."

Mr. Wilder leaned in to ask Principal Akers, "How much? Give me a range." She rested her elbows on the desk, shrugged her shoulders, and frowned her lips. "Um. Anywhere between ten and twenty bucks." Officer Timmons and Mr. Wilder looked up at each other with straight faces. They asked DeSean to wait for them in the sitting area of the front office. DeSean agreed.

After the door was shut, Mr. Wilder looked over his shoulder. He wanted to make sure that DeSean had walked far enough away to not hear him. Mr. Wilder raised his voice. "You know damn well no one can live off twenty dollars a week! Especially not some homeless eighteen-year-old boy who's still wet behind the ears! You should be thanking your lucky stars that he's lasted this long!"

"Come on. Yes, he has a tough situation. But it's not the worst I've seen. Now, the boy who was murdered, LaVeon Kirkland, he had it tough. His mother died during childbirth, and his father was a king-pin. He's serving a forty-five-year sentence right now. But despite being raised by his grandmother, who struggles with Alzheimer's, LaVeon managed to maintain a 4.0 GPA."

Mr. Wilder argued, "We're not talking about LaVeon right now! We're talking about DeSean!"

Officer Timmons followed. "He's right, Ms. Akers." Officer Timmons leaned over her desk to grab a sheet of paper and something to write with. "Look here. Let me do the math for you so you can see for yourself."

Principal Akers sat in her chair, using her feet to push herself away from Officer Timmons. "Um. Okay. But be careful trying to write with those scissors, Officer Timmons."

Officer Timmons stood erect. "Huh? This ain't a ink pen?"

"No, sir. That's a pair of scissors." Mr. Wilder buried his face in his hand silently.

Officer Timmons reacted by tossing the scissors back on the desk. "Well, fuck it then. But you know that man is right. That boy deserves to be getting paid way more than that for all the work he's been doing around here."

Principal Akers addressed Officer Timmons's comment. Her eyes were fixed on Mr. Wilder, who was now staring her in the eyes as well. "Yes, Officer Timmons. You're right. I could've done more." She elevated her voice. "But at least I did something! That's more than I can say for a man who found out and decided to go watch him in the shower!"

Mr. Wilder abruptly stood up. He pointed his index finger at Principal Akers. "I did *not* watch that boy in the shower!"

"Oh yeah? What were you doing, then? Huh?"

Mr. Wilder stuck his chest out. "I was doing what you should've already done—giving that boy a place to stay." Officer Timmons nodded his head silently as he continued to switch his eyes back and forth between the two. Principal Akers stood up and pressed her knuckles down on the table as she leaned forward toward Mr. Wilder.

"Don't you stick your chest out at me, Mr. Wilder! I don't buy your bullshit for one minute! What happened to you being raised by racists and surrounded by Confederate flags your whole life? I suppose now, all of a sudden, you just love black people and want to help!" Officer

Timmons looked at Mr. Wilder with big eyes. He was shocked by what he'd just heard.

"Listen, just because I was raised by racists doesn't mean that I am racist. Fortunately, I have this thing called a brain. I was able to use it. And I realized that treating people unfairly based off the color of their skin is the dumbest thing a human being can do. You could've very well been born black, and Officer Timmons could've been born white. We don't get to pick and choose our appearance or what family we're born into. So I personally believe that anyone who *is* racist is no better than Hitler."

Officer Timmons resumed nodding. Principal Akers offered an apology to Mr. Wilder for her accusations. He accepted it.

"We still have a major issue that needs to be addressed, though." Both men raised their heads.

"What's that?" Mr. Wilder asked.

"The Norfolk Public Schools' bylaws state that a student cannot live with a staff member of his or her respective place of learning unless he or she is the parent of the student or has documentation of parental guardian rights, regardless of age."

Officer Timmons smacked his lips. "Come on, Ms. Akers. I think you can make an exception in this case."

She shrugged her shoulders. "Because I know what happened, I am willing to help as much as possible. But I'm sorry, Officer Timmons, I'm not willing to lose my job over this. I'll see what I can do to work around that rule."

"Thank you," Officer Timmons said.

Mr. Wilder rubbed his chin hairs curiously. "Wait a second. You said you know what happened. What does that mean?" Officer Timmons agreed.

Principal Akers answered, "Well, I know you wouldn't know, Mr. Wilder. But, Officer Timmons, I'm sure you remember the crack house massacre that happened in the Huntersville neighborhood back in early March of this year? Apparently, somebody was on a rampage for money, or drugs, or both. They walked into that crack house and shot all five people in there. Four died, but one lived. DeSean's dad was one of the four who died. His mother was the one who lived."

A grin appeared on Mr. Wilder's face. "Well, that's a sad story. But it's also good news. All I have to do is have the mother sign the papers, and we should be in the clear."

"Not so fast, Mr. Wilder. After his father's passing, they were evicted from their apartment in Ghent a month later. And both of the cars they had were repossessed. This woman doesn't have an address, a cell phone, or even an e-mail."

Mr. Wilder asked, "What type of person doesn't have a phone *or* an address?"

Officer Timmons answered, "A damn crackhead. They don't need all that crap. They communicate through smoke signals."

Principal Akers sensed from the heavy eyebrows and hard exhales that the two men had become frustrated with finding a solution. She dropped her head and put a finger in the air. "One week, Mr. Wilder. I will allow him to stay with you for one week. During that time, you need to find his mother and have her sign those guardian papers."

"Okay. Thank you, Principal Akers."

"Before you go thanking me, you should know that this is a big risk for me. And if I'm questioned by the board this week, I'm not going down alone."

"I understand. But what happens if I can't find his mother?"

"Then maybe he could live with Officer Timmons until he graduates. He's not a staff member."

Officer Timmons mumbled, "I don't think he's going to want to do that."

Principal Akers said, "All right, gentlemen. I think we're done here. Have a nice day."

Near three o'clock in the afternoon, a well-rested Mr. Wilder walked into the school. He whistled his way down the hall toward his classroom. Without warning, as he passed the main office, Principal Akers shoved the door open and whispered aggressively, "Mr. Wilder! I need to see you in my office right now!"

He rolled his eyes and exhaled. Then, he followed Principal Akers into the main office and, finally, into her office. Mr. Wilder shut the door behind himself and took a seat.

"We need to discuss what you are teaching these young men, Mr. Wilder! More specifically, Curtis Jr.!" Principal Akers screamed. She slapped a yellow notebook on her desk and sat down.

Mr. Wilder remained calm. "Why? What happened?"

"Today I received a call from one of his teachers. She requested that I come to her class because of a disturbance. Curtis Jr. was passing this notebook around and had all of the students in the classroom laughing."

Mr. Wilder sat up in his seat. "That's good. He likes to write comedy."

"No! That's not good, Mr. Wilder. He was distracting the other students from learning and preventing the teacher from doing what she is paid to do, which is teach!"

Mr. Wilder tilted his head carelessly while reaching for his cane to stand. "Okay. I'll tell him not to let others read his writing."

Principal Akers raised a finger. "Just a second. That's not the big issue here. After I confiscated his notebook, I read the outline of his novel, which includes a rap. Now, coming from someone who has taken creative writing classes before, I wouldn't consider this work to fall into that category."

Mr. Wilder leaned back in his chair. He held his chin. "So what did it say?"

"Well, it starts off with, 'My dick is so long that I must use the kiddie stall.'"

Mr. Wilder raised his eyebrow. "That sounds a little too proper to be Curtis. Are you sure he used the word 'must'?"

Principle Akers shook her head to signal, "No."

"Well, I need you to read it how he wrote it so that I can make the right assessment." Mr. Wilder reached out. "Or you can just give it to me, and I can read it myself."

Too proud to hand it over, Principal Akers put her hand up. "No. No. That's okay. I'm fully capable of reading it." She coughed to clear her throat. Then she began.

My dick so long that I gotta use the kiddie stall.
My dad hated when he had to buy me custom draws.

My cousin taught me how to strip when I was nineteen.
My first lesson: never dance after collard greens.

I didn't listen. I was glistenin' in Crisco.
Old drunk women's money in my speedo.

My stomach bubbled. I said, "Everybody, back up!"
That night, my stage name became Loose Butt.

Mr. Wilder closed his eyes and pinched them together to keep the tears of laughter from falling.

"So please, tell me what's the 'right' assessment for something like that."

Mr. Wilder gathered himself and collected his thoughts before responding with a straight face. "All be it comedic, I believe all the elements are there for a good storyline. I would say that it's creative writing."

"Excuse me, but a fifty-seven-year-old Asian stripper called Loose Butt trying to turn his life around by becoming a Christian rapper is not exactly what I would call a good story line!"

"Look, Principal Akers, I realize my teaching style is unorthodox. But it's effective, the kids are enjoying it, and, personally, I think they are doing well at it so far."

Principal Akers stood to hand Mr. Wilder Curtis's notebook. "As unorthodox as it may be, you should know that I will be keeping an eye on what you're doing from here on out."

While walking out, Mr. Wilder said, "I understand."

Due to the time spent in Principal Akers's office, Mr. Wilder arrived five minutes late to his class. Jaylen and DeSean playfully teased Mr. Wilder before he could even make it to his desk.

"Uh oh, Mr. Wilder's late. There must be a snowball rolling around in hell right now."

"Yeah, Mr. Wilder. I guess you don't care about creative writing, huh?" The three of them chuckled a bit before Curtis ran into the classroom behind Mr. Wilder. Mr. Wilder handed Curtis his yellow folder as Curtis walked past him.

"A, yo, thanks, Mr. Wilder." Curtis sat in his usual seat.

Mr. Wilder propped his cane up against his desk. "You're welcome. Can you tell me why you're late?"

Curtis shrugged one shoulder nonchalantly. An uncontainable smile covered his face. "Oh, I be hanging out with Officer Timmons sometimes after school. Just joking around mostly, you know."

Mr. Wilder replied, "I understand." He thought, "After the morning I had with Officer Timmons, and the things I learned about him, I think he's the person Curtis should be hanging around."

Mr. Wilder redirected his attention to Jaylen. He couldn't help but notice the unusually large smile on his face. It went well with his fresh haircut and new clothes. "I see somebody's in a good mood today. And wearing some new clothes too," Mr. Wilder commented.

Jaylen giggled. "Yeah. That's 'cause I don't have to go to work today. My dad is coming to pick me up." Jaylen's excitement was so contagious it made everyone in the room smile.

Mr. Wilder nodded. "That's good, Jaylen. I'm glad to see you excited about something for a change." The three teenagers shared a brief laugh.

Mr. Wilder turned to write on the chalkboard "INTRO" as he began to teach. "All right! Today, I'll be teaching you all about introductions. This is the first five to ten pages of your manuscript." As he spoke, Mr. Wilder noticed Jaylen and DeSean hastily taking notes. Curtis, however, sat with his hands in his pockets. His yellow notebook was closed on his desk. "Are you relying on your memory today, Curtis?" Mr. Wilder stopped to ask.

Curtis turned to face Mr. Wilder. He shrugged his shoulders. "Nah. It just ain't no need in me taking notes when today is my last day."

DeSean slammed his pen on his desk.

Jaylen shouted, "For what?"

Mr. Wilder tossed the small piece of chalk back on the shelf. "What are you talking about, Curtis?"

"A, yo, Mr. Wilder. I ain't trying to disturb the class with all this. But I told you my dad ain't feelin' me doing this creative writing stuff. He says it's a waste of time and that my time would be better spent getting in shape for ROTC. Then, when he got the call today about me getting my notebook taken by the principal for disrupting the class, that just put him over the edge. I mean, you can talk to my mom about it when she come pick me up today. But that's really all I have to say."

Mr. Wilder responded, "Okay. I'll do that."

DeSean commented, "Man, I'm sorry to hear that, Curtis."

Jaylen now had a straight face. "Yeah, me too."

"All right! Let's regain focus, everybody!" Mr. Wilder raised his voice to say. He limped over to Curtis's desk without his cane, bent over, and whispered in his ear, "And, Curtis, you should still be taking notes just in case my discussion with your parents goes as planned." Curtis reached for his pen to begin writing.

Mr. Wilder stood to make his way back to his desk. He assumed his usual position of leaning against it and then addressed the class. "Now, as I was saying earlier about introduction, better known as the 'intro' to your novel: this is the first five to ten pages of your manuscript and, to be blunt about it, your opportunity to get the reader's attention. It's a proven fact that if a reader's interest isn't peaked in the first five to ten pages, the likelihood of him or her finishing that book drops at least 50 percent."

Curtis interrupted him. "A, yo, Mr. Wilder. What about the cover, though? My cover gonna be so sick, people gonna have to pick it up and read it."

Jaylen followed. "Yeah. And what about all that shit on the back of the book where people tell you everything that's going to happen?"

Mr. Wilder answered, "Well, the short answer to both of you all's questions is 'bullshit' and 'bullshit.'" DeSean laughed. Curtis and Jaylen sat up in their seats to listen closer. "Now, here's the long answer. I'll start with you first, Curtis, and your 'sick' cover. You're right. A great cover can attract a lot of attention and even cause people to pick it up. But it ends there. If a reader decides to pick up your book based off its cover, then the cover has done its job, and you should keep that same artist for all of your novels. However, the last time I checked, they don't give awards for the best book cover. And readers don't come to book stores looking for great pieces of art. They're looking for a great story!"

Curtis leaned back in his seat. Mr. Wilder switched his attention to Jaylen. "And, Jaylen, all that 'shit' on the back of the book is better known as the synopsis. And, for the record, a synopsis does *not* tell the reader everything that is going to happen. That would be like me telling you everything that is going to happen in a movie. Would you still want to go watch it?"

Jaylen shook his head. "No."

Mr. Wilder responded, "I didn't think so. The purpose of the synopsis is to let the potential reader know the setting, the problem, and maybe a few of the adversities the protagonist will face. It does not tell the solution to the problem. It does not tell the ending. It does not give any details. And it certainly does not let the reader know whether he or she will like the author's writing style. You still have to open the book and read it for that. If the synopsis is well written, the reader will give the book a chance by, again, reading the first five to ten pages." Jaylen dropped his head and started scratching it.

Mr. Wilder resumed. "The only question left on the table is, how do I capture the reader in the first five to ten pages? The answer is, there are many different ways. Some people like to start with action. Some like to start with passion. Some like to start with conflict. Some like to start with a good joke. Hell, some like to start subtle, giving the false appearance of normality so that it is easy for the reader to relate. Then, all hell breaks loose. The bottom line is this, guys: you have to find what works best for you *and* your story."

Jaylen raised his hand. "Hey, Mr. Wilder. I've been meaning to talk to you about that too. I'm struggling with my story a lil' bit."

"What about it?"

Jaylen used hand gestures. "The ending. You remember how my story had to do with the father and son invading China, right?" Mr. Wilder nodded.

"Well, I always watch war movies and action movies. In those, all the good guys end up walking away unharmed after their shoot outs and battles. I just think that it makes it unrealistic. So I'm trying to find a way to end it where the father and son realize through a couple of physical mishaps that all they have to rely on in life is each other."

As the classroom phone rang, Mr. Wilder replied, "It sounds like you just answered your own question, Jaylen. All you have to do now is figure out what those physical mishaps will be."

With a grin on his face, Jaylen stood up and grabbed his book bag to leave. "That's my dad calling to tell me he's outside. I'll see y'all next week."

Mr. Wilder went to the corner of the room closest to the entry door and answered the black phone that hung on the wall. "Wilder speaking."

"Hi, Mr. Wilder. This Ms. Tonya, Jaylen's mother." Mr. Wilder raised his index finger to stop Jaylen from walking out.

"Listen, I'm on my work phone, so I can't talk long. But I just wanted to let you know that Jaylen *will* be needing a ride from you today. His father just called and told me he won't be able to make it. His sorry ass ain't even give me a reason this time. He just said something came up. Then, when I tried to tell him to call Jaylen himself, he hung up the phone."

Mr. Wilder looked up at Jaylen. He stood at the doorway with a playful smile. "Would you like me to tell him?"

After Jaylen heard Mr. Wilder say that, he stopped smiling, took off his book bag, and shoved it back on his desk. Mr. Wilder said, "Just a second, ma'am. Jaylen, the phone's for you."

Jaylen smacked his lips as he snatched the phone from Mr. Wilder. "Yeah, big surprise. Hello. Hey, ma…yes, ma'am. I know…yes, ma'am. I got it, a cup of noodles…I love you too." Jaylen's head hung low. He slammed the phone back on the hook.

Mr. Wilder leaned with his back against the blackboard. His thumbs were dipped in his pant pockets. Curtis and DeSean sat quietly, trying not to make eye contact with Jaylen. The room was so quiet, every little squeak from the old desks and chairs sounded amplified.

Mr. Wilder said calmly, "I'm sorry, Jaylen."

Jaylen swiftly walked back to his desk, yanked out his notebook, and began writing. "It ain't nothing to be sorry about, Mr. Wilder. What you sorry for? That motherfucka is dead is all!"

"Whoa now, Jaylen! Let's not take this too far."

Jaylen continued to press down hard on his paper. He wrote rapidly. "I don't know what you're talkin' about, Mr. Wilder. I'm just talking about writing. This is a creative writing class, ain't it? I couldn't decide how to end my story. Now I'm telling you the father is going to fuckin' die! And it's going to be the most graphic fuckin' shit you ever read in your goddamn life!"

Mr. Wilder sympathized. "I understand."

Jaylen threw his pen against the wall, jumped up, and walked toward Mr. Wilder. "Do you really fuckin' understand? Do you understand that I walked three blocks in the fuckin' rain yesterday to get this haircut! Do you understand that sometimes I don't even get $200 a week from my job! And most of that goes to help my mom with the bills! I spent the rest of my check on these fuckin' clothes and haircut...for him!"

Jaylen stood face-to-face with Mr. Wilder. Tears flowed down his face effortlessly. "Do you have any idea how this shit feels, Mr. Wilder? It fuckin' hurts!" Mr. Wilder wrapped his arms tightly around Jaylen. Jaylen continued to cry as he laid his head on Mr. Wilder's shoulder with his fists clenched shut.

"What's wrong with me, huh? What the fuck is wrong with me? I do good in school! I work! And I take care of my mama and lil' sister! Why is he so ashamed of me, Mr. Wilder? I'm his fuckin' son! And he doesn't even want to fuckin' see me!"

5

With the onset of autumn, there was a slight breeze in the air. The leaves that had fallen slid across the parking lot asphalt. Mr. Wilder stood on the curb next to Jaylen. Curtis opened the door to his mother's SUV and sat in the front passenger seat.

Mr. Wilder wondered aloud, "Um. I thought you were supposed to be driving as much as possible, Curtis?"

Curtis smacked his lips. "Yeah, I know. Just another perk my dad took away from me for that incident that happened in school today." Curtis's comment reminded Mr. Wilder that he wanted to set up a time to meet with Curtis's dad. Mr. Wilder shot his hand up in the air to grab Curtis's mother's attention. He limped as fast as he could over to the driver-side window.

Mrs. Jordan rolled down her window to speak. "Hi, Mr. Wilder. I guess you heard about everything that happened today."

"Yes. The principal put me up to speed on the incident that took place in the classroom today and—"

Without warning, the school doors flung open. DeSean came out, jumping off the steps and curb. He walked rapidly through the parking lot. The sheer noise and action alone was enough to grab everyone's attention. But Mr. Wilder thought, "Where could he possibly be going? He's supposed to be coming with me."

Mr. Wilder shouted across the parking lot, "Hey! Where are you going?"

DeSean turned his face, but not his body, as he continued to walk away. "Haha! I'm going home, Mr. Wilder! Duh!"

Mr. Wilder briefly squinted his eyes in wonder. He wanted to chase DeSean down and demand a straight answer. But he knew that wasn't the time or place, nor was he even physically capable of doing so.

Mrs. Jordan regained his attention. "Is everything all right, Mr. Wilder?"

"Yes. Yes, Mrs. Jordan. Listen, I would like to sit down with you and your husband sometime this week to talk about Curtis."

"I really think that's a great idea, Mr. Wilder. But you probably already know that I had nothing to do with the decision to take Jr. out of your class. That was all my husband's doing. We discuss everything together, but the final decision is his. He's the leader of our household. Plus, he's not going to come up to the school to talk about this. You're going to have to come to him."

Mr. Wilder nodded. "I understand. That's fine. Just give me a time and a place, and I'll be there."

"Well, the only time I can guarantee he'll be available is early in the morning next Wednesday. His schedule is slam packed every day leading up to then."

"How early are we talking? And where at?"

She looked Mr. Wilder in the eyes with a grin. "That would be at our house at six o'clock in the morning."

Mr. Wilder didn't flinch a muscle. "Well, I hate that Curtis is going to have to miss next Tuesday, but that's fine."

Curtis's mother wrote their address down on a spare napkin and handed it to Mr. Wilder. "Here you go. I'll let him know to expect you."

Mr. Wilder backed up to let Mrs. Jordan drive away. "Thank you."

Mr. Wilder waved Jaylen over to get in the car so they could leave. Jaylen was still angry about his father not coming. He dragged his feet and hung his head on the way to the car. Mr. Wilder unlocked the doors. Jaylen hopped in and closed the passenger door. Mr. Wilder was in the process of raising his leg to get in when he heard a stern voice coming from behind him.

"Hey."

Mr. Wilder was startled. He turned quickly to respond to the man. "Hey! Can I help you?"

It was the same janitor who'd stared at Mr. Wilder numerous times before as he left the school's parking lot.

"Yeah. The name's Jim Adams," the man said as he briefly removed his hands from his hips to point at the sewn-in name tag on his shirt. "Everybody around here just calls me Jawbone. I'm a man of few words. So I like to keep my mouth shut."

Mr. Wilder interrupted him by extending his hand. "Mr. Wilder, Jawbone. It's good to meet you."

Jawbone glanced down at Mr. Wilder's hand while he kept his hands rested on his hips. "You can put your hand away. I know who you are." Mr. Wilder squinted his eyes at the janitor and slowly put his arm back down along his side. "Like I said, I don't talk much, so I hear a lot. I just came over to tell you that you're wasting your time with these little black boys. Those little black bastards don't give a damn about no books. Hell, at that age all they care about is drugs, sex, and occasionally money if there's some to be made. Then when they get to be grown, all they're going to care about is money, drugs, and occasionally sex if there's some to be had. Besides, what you care about these future criminals for, anyway?"

Jawbone's negative attitude left a nasty taste in Mr. Wilder's mouth. "Jawbone, I think this conversation, along with any other future conversations, is over between you and me."

Jawbone took two steps back. "I understand. But do you mind if I ask what happened to your leg?"

"In fact, I do mind. Now, I suggest that you get out of my way before I start driving. We wouldn't want an 'accident' to happen, now would we?"

Jawbone kept his eyes on Mr. Wilder as he walked backward toward the school's entrance.

Mr. Wilder got in the car and started the engine.

Jaylen asked, "Who was that?"

Mr. Wilder adjusted his rearview mirror. He looked back at the janitor who stood in front of the school, still staring at his car. "I don't know, Jaylen. Just some confused old black man."

As the car began to move, Jaylen didn't hesitate to ask, "Hey, Mr. Wilder. I was planning on asking my dad. But I was wondering if you could explain the advice you gave me last time about girls. You know, when you told me to lie."

A grin came over Mr. Wilder's face. "That was just my erratic response to the plans you told me you had with her."

"Oh." Jaylen dropped his head.

"Now, wait a minute, Jaylen. I don't want you to start feeling bad for wanting to have sex with that girl. That's natural. Hell, at some point in time every man will see a woman he wants to have sex with. The real problem is that you don't realize what sex is. That's why you don't feel like you're too young for it."

"No. I took the sex ed. course where they separate all the boys from the girls."

Mr. Wilder's grin grew into a smile. "That's not what I was referring to, Jaylen. Those classes only talk about the physical act of sex, how to protect yourself, and the consequences if you don't. They don't teach what sex really is."

"What is it?"

"Sex is just the physical expression of an emotional bond. Now, I know things have been screwed up with prostitution and pornography. But that's what sex really is. So when I originally said to be yourself, I meant taking the time to talk to her and telling her the things you like. Showing her the things you like. Learning things she likes. Doing things she likes. Bond with her. Develop a friendship. Care for, trust, and respect each other. Then, your heart will be in the right place. And you will want to do right by her by waiting until you're married."

"What? Man, my friends ain't got to go through all that to have sex."

"Yeah, well, there's a big difference between a boy having sex with a girl and a man making love with a woman."

Jaylen looked down and scratched his head. Mr. Wilder put the car in park in front of Jaylen's apartment. "Hey, thanks for the ride, Mr. Wilder."

"No problem. Think about what I said."

"Yeah. Okay. I will." Jaylen got out and closed the door gently before walking away.

It was nearly dark outside as Mr. Wilder arrived at his apartment complex. He parked in his usual space directly behind the Church's Chicken drive-through menu. He got out of his car and looked over to his left. Mr. Wilder saw DeSean sitting on the curb next to an industrial-sized garbage container, eating a piece of chicken.

"DeSean?"

"Man, it's about time you showed up, Mr. Wilder. I was starting to think you reneged on me like they did back in the day with those forty acres."

Mr. Wilder rolled his eyes. "Oh boy. Here we go with that again."

DeSean smiled. "Nah, I'm just playing."

"Good. Because I thought you had backed out of the deal when you told me you were going home earlier."

"No. You told me I could stay with you. So this is my home now."

Mr. Wilder nodded. "So I see you bought yourself some dinner."

"Nope. I got this chicken for free. While I was sitting out here waiting for you, some dude came out here with an apron on and a box full of chicken in his hands. He was walking to the trashcan. So I asked him what he was about to do. He said he was 'bout to throw it all away because they not allowed to serve food that's been sitting out for longer than two hours. It could become unsanitary at that point."

"I see that didn't bother you, though."

"Hell naw! I told him to give me that unsanitized shit. I'll eat it."

Mr. Wilder grinned. He watched DeSean take another bite of the fried chicken that dripped grease on the asphalt below.

"So should I be expecting you to come home every night around this time? I mean, that's not a problem if so. I'll just go find something to do."

"Yes, I usually get home about this time every Tuesday. I take Jaylen to work or home after each class. You could ride with us, if you'd like, so you don't have to worry about finding something to do."

"Okay, cool. That sounds good."

"All right. Let's get inside. Where are your bags?"

DeSean picked up his book bag and swung it over his shoulder. He looked at Mr. Wilder with a smile. "This is it."

Mr. Wilder led the way, leaning heavily on the wooden rails leading up to his third-floor apartment. He struggled to get his key in the door due to the poorly lit stairway. After stepping on the hard, beige, linoleum floor, DeSean closed the door behind himself. He looked around at the nearly empty, bare-walled apartment.

"For someone who is retired and ballin' like you say you are, this sure is a crappy apartment. Everything is outdated. And you ain't got but one couch facing a small desk with a typewriter on it. Wait a minute. Is that a battery-operated TV on the kitchen counter?"

Mr. Wilder nodded. "Yes, it is. I use it from time to time to watch the news. And I told you before, in class, looks don't—"

DeSean cut him off while rolling his eyes. "Yeah. Yeah. Yeah. I know. Looks don't matter. Don't focus on looking like the man. Focus on being the man. Your money always looks better in your bank account. But still, though, you could be living nicer than this, Mr. Wilder."

"And you could be fucking homeless right now, DeSean."

DeSean paused. "Yeah, you're right. I'm sorry about that, Mr. Wilder. Oh, and thanks again for letting me stay here. I really do appreciate it."

"Not a problem at all." Mr. Wilder pointed. "Now, that's my bedroom over there. And that's the one and only bathroom in this apartment right there beside it. Don't ever disturb me while I'm in either of the two. Is that clear?"

"Yes, sir. That's clear."

"Good. You'll be sleeping out here on the couch. There's a blanket and a pillow in the linen closet that you can use. Oh, and there's another typewriter in my room. So feel free to use this set up out here to do your homework and write your book. The bottom drawer is full of fresh paper. And the top drawer has notepads, ink pens, and pencils in case you need to jot down any notes."

DeSean looked over at the shiny black typewriter with gold trim. "Wow. Thanks, Mr. Wilder. Are you sure? That typewriter looks expensive."

Mr. Wilder grinned. "That's because it is expensive. I don't mind spending money on things I need. As a writer, the worst thing in the world is having a good idea and not having the resources to write it. But yes, I'm sure that you can use it. I have a similar set up in my bedroom."

DeSean wondered aloud, "Okay, cool. But if you don't mind spending money on the things you use to write, why does that desk chair look so worn down? It has duct tape on it and some big red stain."

Mr. Wilder thought, "Boy, this kid asks a lot of questions." He placed his hand on top of the beige, cloth office chair. "That's because I'm also a little superstitious. I wrote my first fifteen books in this chair, although none of them were ever published. I still feel that they were great stories. This chair constantly reminds me that I write because I love to, not because of the money or someone else thinking that I'm good at it."

"So you said you wrote fifteen books in that chair, and none of them got published?"

"That's right."

Picking up the typewriter and setting it on the floor, DeSean mumbled, "Ain't no way in hell I'm using that chair." Mr. Wilder couldn't make out what he'd said. He asked DeSean to repeat himself.

"I said I prefer to sit on the floor when I type. I'm more comfortable down there."

"Okay. Suit yourself. I'm going to go put my things in my room."

DeSean walked to the refrigerator and opened it. He saw a half-eaten sandwich, a nearly empty bottle of mustard, and an open box of baking soda. DeSean shook his head and tried the freezer. All he found was three blue ice trays off to the left, and they weren't even full.

The sound of Mr. Wilder's footsteps grew louder as he approached. DeSean closed the freezer door and stood up to face him.

"Are you already hungry again?"

"No, and it's a good thing that I'm not. You don't have anything to eat in there."

"I know. When I get hungry, I run out and buy myself something to eat. It's not a big deal."

"Maybe not for you. But what about me?"

Mr. Wilder waved DeSean off. He grabbed himself a glass of water from the faucet.

"Don't try to feed me that poor-boy bullshit. You might not have enough money to afford a roof over your head, but I know you've been working and getting paid under the table by that principal down at school."

DeSean dropped his head. After a quick thought, he rushed to speak. "Yeah, but I'm not trying to spend that money on food, though. It's just like you always say: 'Be smart with your money.' So how about I make a deal with you?"

Mr. Wilder sipped his water. "I'm listening."

"I will cook and keep the house clean if you buy the groceries. That will keep me from having to spend all my money on food. And you will be saving a lot of money, as opposed to going out to eat every night. What do you think about that?"

"You've got yourself a deal." They looked at each other in the eyes as they shook on it.

Lightheartedly, Mr. Wilder said, "I guess I should be getting ready for high cholesterol and high blood pressure with all this fried food I'm about to be eating."

DeSean chuckled. "Contrarily, I don't know how to fry anything. I either bake, sauté, steam, or grill all my foods."

Mr. Wilder cut his eyes at him. "Whoa. You're a black guy from Norfolk, and you don't know how to fry anything? And you correctly pronounced 'contrarily'?"

DeSean laughed again. "It might make more sense if I told you I was from Ghent."

Mr. Wilder smiled. "That still doesn't help. But how'd you end up in this situation?"

DeSean turned his lips while thinking momentarily. "We'll get back to that. I feel like you know enough about me already. But I don't know anything about you."

"What do you want to know?"

"For starters, since I'm going to be living here and everything, I want to know if you're into any crazy stuff, like killing people and hiding them in the freezer? Kidnapping people? Sexually trying to take advantage of people? Particularly young teenage boys?"

Mr. Wilder raised his hand with a smile. "Okay, I get your point. You can stop. You want to know if I'm crazy. The answer is no. In fact, the longer you live here, the more you'll realize that I prefer being left alone."

"Okay, good."

"Do you have any other questions?"

"Yeah, just one more, for now. I noticed on the side of that desk over there that you have a picture taped to it. I also noticed that you're not wearing a wedding band. So I wanted to know if that's your baby mama and son?"

Mr. Wilder closed his eyes while shaking his head with a grin. "No, that's my ex-wife and, technically, my stepson, although I call him my son."

"That's cool. She's a pretty lady. I'm surprised you married a blonde, though. You seem like the intellectual type."

Mr. Wilder snickered. "You're telling me. You should've seen the look on my mother's face when I brought her home for the first time."

"So do they have names?"

"Oh, yeah. Allison and Conner."

There was an awkward moment of silence before DeSean began making circles with his hand.

"Annnd…"

"And what?"

"And why did you guys get divorced? Where are they now? Why are you here and not trying to get them back? Tell me the whole story. I want to know everything."

Mr. Wilder took a deep breath and exhaled hard, thinking, "I should've never told him he could ask me anything." Mr. Wilder walked to the living room and flopped on the couch.

"Okay, DeSean. Have a seat in that desk chair over there, and I'll tell you all about it." DeSean followed Mr. Wilder's footsteps back to the living room.

He had a quick thought about Mr. Wilder's fifteen unpublished books and said, "No, that's okay. I'll just stand."

Mr. Wilder shrugged his shoulders. "Everything I'm about to tell you all happened over the course of about ten years. But to me, it felt like it all happened just like that." Mr. Wilder snapped his fingers. "After I graduated from Bridgewater College, I was working as a night-shift manager at Pilgrim's Pride Chicken right outside of Harrisonburg, Virginia. That's where we met. She was a truck driver. We used to call them 'transporters' down at the plant. I'll never forget the first time I laid eyes on her. Her blond hair was blowing all over her face. And they could never find a uniform that fit her petite stature the right way. They always fit like a child wearing her parent's clothes. Even with all that, though, she couldn't hide that million-dollar smile. I'm telling you, I'da cut my own heart out of my chest and handed it to her if she'd asked for it."

Mr. Wilder cleared his throat. "To make a long story short, we ended up dating for a few months, and then we got married. Conner was eight years old when we got married. She'd had him in a previous relationship. So there I was at twenty-two years old, married into a ready-made family, broke, and not knowing the first thing to do. Fortunately, there was an older guy at my job who pulled me to the side and taught me about the stock market. Because of his advice, I was able to retire ten years later, which was about twenty-five years sooner than I was planning to."

DeSean interrupted him. "Wait a minute. I realize you were in love and everything. But why would you rush to get married into a ready-made family knowing you were broke in the first place?"

"You don't understand. I loved to write, and I still do. Allison loved that I loved to write. She would stay up late just to read my books. Hell, she was the inspiration for most of them. So I rushed to marry her because she was the first person I'd ever met who truly understood me. But it wasn't until after being married for a few years that I noticed Conner starting to take a liking to writing as well. Initially, I thought it was because he'd seen me writing all the time and was following in my footsteps. Then I learned that no stepfather is that lucky. His biological father was a screenwriter for major production company and had been doing pretty well for himself. Then he had hit a dry spell where he couldn't think of any good movie ideas. Allison told me that he'd tried liquor at first. Then it had become drugs. And, eventually, one time, it had led to abuse. That's when she grabbed her son, packed up all their things, and moved to Virginia with her mother."

"So, if everything was so good between y'all, why'd y'all get divorced?"

"Well, we both retired from the chicken plant five days after we celebrated our ten-year wedding anniversary. She knew that I really wanted to take a shot at becoming a professional writer. But she didn't like the person I'd become in retirement. Although I never did any drinking, drugs, or, God knows, abuse, she claims that my attitude reminded her a lot of her ex and that my love for writing was making me stir crazy. Even though he wrote screenplays and I write novels, I can tell you that there *is* a dark side to writing. I'm talking about tons and tons of rejection letters after you've slaved over a manuscript for a whole year. I'm talking about you spending your hard-earned money on an editor just so they can tell you not to quit your fucking day job.

"So, yes, after I retired, I shopped a few of my manuscripts around. I received a ton of rejection letters and was always angry because of it. Now, I realize that as a writer, you have to have tough skin. But there's only so much that a man can take. When I think about it, I'm at peace with our divorce. Allison had every right to leave me. I was miserable to be around. Conner was in college when Allison left me to move back with her mother. I hear she's remarried now."

"Let me guess. To another writer?"

Mr. Wilder chuckled. "A playwright in New York."

DeSean laughed. "So what about Conner?"

"When his mother and I split, he'd gotten arrested for underage drinking in college. I went over to the school and bailed him out, as usual. I feel like all I ever did was bail him out of trouble his whole life. He was the type who never seemed to grow up. I haven't heard anything from him since, though. I'm sure he still loves to write. And if he stays focused, he'll succeed at it. He doesn't have as many obstacles in front of him as I did. I'll try to call him from time to time, but he doesn't answer. And I'm not surprised. We never had a true father-and-son relationship, even though I tried hard to. He wanted that relationship with his biological father, but he never got it. Conner knows I'm only a call away if he needs me, though."

DeSean scratched his head. "Okay, all of that makes sense. But what the hell are you doing here?"

"I told you I made a lot of money in the stock market. Then I got divorced. Allison took half of everything. And half of a lot equals enough. So I keep working small jobs here and there. Nothing strenuous, just enough to pay my bills without having to come out of my savings. When I saw the position open at the school, I thought it was right up my alley. I love creative writing, and it was something that wouldn't require a lot out of me."

DeSean silently nodded.

Mr. Wilder asked, "Do you have any other questions for me before you tell me how a young black man from Ghent who can't even fry chicken ends up in your situation?"

DeSean rapidly turned his head and snapped his fingers. "Dang! I thought I'd asked you enough questions to forget about that…or, at least, not be in the mood to talk anymore."

Mr. Wilder put his hands behind his head with a smile. "Nope. I don't forget much. And it's rare that I have company, so I'm in the mood to talk."

DeSean smacked his lips. "I don't know what you're asking me for, anyway. I know Principal Akers already told you what happened."

"Yes, but she only gave me a summary. And, like you said earlier about me, 'I want to know everything.'"

DeSean fell on the opposite side of the couch, away from Mr. Wilder. "It all started last year. My parents and I lived in a condo in Ghent. My mom was a stay-at-home mom. My dad would come pick me up after school when he got off work. Usually, dinner would be waiting for us when we walked through the door. But it was around that time that she started scrambling to make dinner when we came home. Then, she started coming home the same time we came home. Then, it was all the arguments with my dad wondering where she'd been. Eventually, we only saw her three to four times a week. Even then, it was late at night, and things started coming up missing around the house.

"One day, when my dad and I got home, we saw this little dude, smaller than me, with a real thick beard sitting on our couch, eating a big-ass bowl of cereal and watching a pay-per-view special. He had a gun sitting in his lap too. He told my dad that my mom owed him $700. I don't think my dad even blinked before he reached in his pocket to pay him from the ball of money he had. That day, my dad changed all the locks on the condo. He told me that I was no longer allowed to let my mother in.

"Then, we drove to this rehab place where my dad reserved a spot for my mom. He even paid a $2,000 deposit. So then we drove around trying to find my mom. My dad recognized the guy's motorcycle from earlier and walked in the crack house where it was parked. He told me to stay in the car. About ten seconds later, my dad came out, running to the car. He swung the door open and reached under the driver's seat for his pistol. He was about to slam the door shut and run into the house again. But he doubled back to ask me, 'You know I love you, right, Son?'

"Of course I said yes because I knew my dad loved me. But that was the first time I'd ever looked into my dad's eyes with fear of what he might do next. When he walked into the house for the second time, he closed the door behind himself. I heard seven shots go off. I was afraid for a moment, but I had to figure out what was going on. I got out of the car and slowly approached the front door. As I grabbed the knob, another shot rang out. It was almost deafening. I'd never heard a gunshot that close before. I remember the door being hard as hell to push open. I still couldn't hear anything, but I just kept saying 'Dad! It's me, DeSean!' over and over so he wouldn't shoot.

"The smell of that house was awful. There were holes, dents, and scratches on the walls. The carpet was so stained I couldn't even tell what color it was. The first thing I did was look behind the door to my left to see what was blocking it. There was a dead man, who'd been shot in the neck, laid out in a growing puddle of blood. Across the living room, sitting on the floor with his back against the wall, was another guy who'd been shot in the chest and died. Straight ahead was the kitchen, where I saw someone's bare feet upside down on the floor. The rest of that person's body was hidden behind the cabinets.

"I started yelling louder for my dad as I tiptoed toward the kitchen. When I peeked over the counter, I saw the small guy from earlier lying on his back, dead. He'd been shot in the head and neck. But there was a woman who'd been shot three times in the lower back, face down on the floor with her head in his lap. I walked around the counter to get a better look of who the woman was. Surprise. Surprise. It was my mom. And the dude's pants were unzipped with his dick out right beside her forehead. My dad obviously walked in on her giving that dude a blow-job. The blood on the tile floor in the kitchen was starting to spread toward me, so I jumped back into the living room. Seeing my mom laying there like that made me cry. I just wanted to run out of there and wait back in the car for my dad.

"When I opened the door to leave, the sunlight lit up the hallway to my left. That's where my dad was stretched out on his back. His brains were splattered across the floor and walls. The only way I knew it was him was because I remembered the clothes he had on. I ran all the way home. I didn't eat anything for two days. Apparently, someone showed up to the house after me, but before the police, because the police report says that everyone's pockets were empty. But I know for a fact my dad had cash on him."

Mr. Wilder's lips were tight and his fists were balled in anger.

DeSean noticed his demeanor. "What's wrong, Mr. Wilder?"

Mr. Wilder struggled to keep a calm tone. "You told me a true story."

"Yeah, everything I just told you is true."

Mr. Wilder waved him off. "I'm not talking about that! Yeah, you had some rough circumstances, but I'm talking about your novel! When you read your story line in class, that was your true story?"

"Yeah. So what?"

"So what! So what! That's a fucking autobiography, is what! Who the fuck are you? Nobody wants to read the autobiography of some no-name high schooler! No matter how sui generis his story is! And here's a question for you: How the fuck is the story going to end, huh? With you living with a middle-aged white guy? You need to think of a story! Something with a beginning, middle, and end! You need a plot, a twist, a climax, etcetera! Remember, it's creative writing, not truthful writing. Get famous, and *then* write your autobiography for millions!"

DeSean bit his lip and looked up to think. "Okay, I can do that. But don't try to pin all this shit on me like I'm a dumbass. You're the fucking teacher! You should've gave better instructions!"

Mr. Wilder sighed. "Ok, dually noted. But before you get too deep in thought about it, tell me why you didn't go live with any of your extended family."

"What extended family? All my grandparents are dead. And my mom is an only child. My dad supposedly has a brother who lives in Richmond, but I never met him. He didn't even show up to the funeral. My dad never invited him over because he's gay. He had no tolerance for the alternative lifestyle. He used to say that they were a bunch of confused people, acting unnaturally, and it had no place in his home. Besides, since my mom survived, everyone thought that it would be me and her living together now. But after she got out of the hospital, she wasn't even home for a week before she started running back out in the streets. I did like my dad and changed the locks again. But eventually, the little money I'd gotten from his death had dwindled away, and I got evicted. Now, here I am. I have a bigger check coming when I turn twenty-five, though."

"That's always nice."

DeSean responded with a grin. "Yeah."

"When's the last time you saw your mother?"

"This morning before school."

"What?"

"Yeah. I usually sleep under the highway in front of Harbor Park. There's no traffic at night, so it's quiet. Plus, there's no bugs because it's concrete with no food around. So to get to school, I usually take the underpass on Brambleton Avenue. Every other way puts me on Tidewater Drive longer than I want to be. Out there, everybody can see you walking to school, and I don't need all those people in my business. But yeah, the underpass on Brambleton is where I saw her sleeping at this morning. It's right before you get to the 7-Eleven shopping center across from Norfolk State. She's usually sleeping there every morning. I don't know where she goes while I'm at school. But at night, she's on Church Street trying to get money for drugs."

Mr. Wilder stood abruptly. "Oh, good! Now all we have to do is interrupt her and have her sign the papers." Mr. Wilder began to walk toward the door.

DeSean rushed to cut him off. "Whoa! Hold up, Mr. Wilder! What type of work do you think she's doing? And what papers are you talking about?"

Mr. Wilder reached down in his pocket and grabbed the guardian papers to show, DeSean. "Listen to me, DeSean. I need your mother to sign these guardian papers so that you can continue to live here legally."

"Okay, that makes sense."

"Good. Now I'm assuming that your mother is probably working to help keep the sanctuaries clean at night over there on Church Street."

DeSean laughed. "No, sir, Mr. Wilder. Church Street ain't no holy place…especially at night. They got hookers, both male and female, out there."

"What? I've never known a gigolo to stand out on the street like a hooker."

"That's 'cause they're not gigolos, Mr. Wilder. These men are dressed like women."

"What do you mean? Like drag?"

"No, sir. In drag, at least the guys resemble women. Those dudes on Church Street be looking like Bob Sapp in a halter top. I *really* think we should wait and try to catch her before she gets to Church Street at night."

"Okay. But it needs to happen by next Tuesday!"

"I understand. I want this to happen too, Mr. Wilder. We're going to get it done, and I'm going to help you."

"Okay."

DeSean flopped back down on the couch with a smile. "So what should I call you now, since we'll be living together? I think 'Mr. Wilder' sounds too formal." Still standing, Mr. Wilder's head snapped back. He was offended by the question.

"You can, and will continue to, call me Mr. Wilder. You'll be leaving this home after the school year ends, just like every other eighteen-year-old high-school graduate. Our relationship is still, and will remain, that of a teacher and student. The only reason I decided to let you stay with me is because I feel like everyone deserves to at least have a roof over their heads all the way up through high school so they can have a decent start at life."

DeSean nodded. Mr. Wilder continued. "I suggest you get started writing for that $60,000. I think that'll make moving out seem a lot easier."

DeSean slid down to the floor from the couch. He sat in front of the typewriter and began to type.

6

The following Tuesday, Mr. Wilder barged into the classroom with less than a minute to spare before being considered late. He immediately looked toward the desks and noticed Curtis was absent. Mr. Wilder dropped his head and shook it, and then turned toward his desk. His body language expressed his emotional letdown. Mr. Wilder was alarmed as he nearly walked into Principle Akers. She stood there, leaning on the edge of the desk with her arms crossed.

She impatiently tapped her foot on the floor. She glanced down at her watch before looking up at Mr. Wilder. "You're cutting it close, Mr. Wilder."

Mr. Wilder didn't feel the need to respond. He stood there with his hands overlapping, waiting for Principal Akers to explain why she was in his classroom.

Her foot continued to tap as her face grew redder by the second. "I guess being in class and prepared to teach before three thirty is too much to ask from someone who seems to have started a writing gang in my school."

"Excuse me?" Mr. Wilder asked.

Principal Akers looked toward Jaylen. "Do you want to tell him, or do you want me to do it, Jaylen?"

Jaylen shrugged his shoulders carelessly. He looked up at Mr. Wilder. "I got in a fight today."

Principal Akers coughed. Jaylen corrected himself. "I mean, *we* got in a fight today."

"For what?" Mr. Wilder asked.

"That dude Victor Brown from the football team started it. Me, DeSean, and Curtis was sitting at our table in the cafeteria writing and minding our business. Then, Victor comes over there questioning why he saw DeSean out Mission College apartments last night. So DeSean tells him that his peoples moved out there and that's where he stayin' now. Victor ain't believe him, so he kept buggin'. But DeSean just ignored him. Then Victor got frustrated, so he snatched DeSean's notebook he was writing on. And he threw it on that nasty-ass cafeteria floor."

Principal Akers cut in. "Jaylen, watch your language, please."

Jaylen apologized. "My bad, Ms. Akers. He threw it on that *filthy-ass* cafeteria floor." Jaylen watched Principal Akers and Mr. Wilder both shake their heads.

"What?" Jaylen asked.

Mr. Wilder answered, "Nothing, Jaylen. Just finish your story."

DeSean sat at his desk with a smirk on his face as Jaylen resumed. "Okay. Anyway, that's when Curtis started going in on Victor and telling him to give DeSean his notebook back. First, Curtis was like, 'Victor, how you gonna be captain of the football team when you haven't made a tackle or a touchdown? That's why we can't win no games now.'

Everybody in the cafeteria was rollin'. And you know Victor real thick from lifting weights all the time, so Curtis said his neck was shaped like a box of cereal. He really started getting under Victor's skin when he started jonin' on his girl, though. Her name is Tilisha, but everybody just calls her Twinkie. Curtis said her nickname should be Jiffy, 'cause she got kankles thick as cornbread. Then Curtis asked her how she got the nerve to wear some Apple Bottom jeans with her flat butt. Tilisha was like, 'I don't know what you talking about, Curtis. My butt big!' Curtis said, 'Nah, you right. You should be wearing Apple Bottom jeans, 'cause yo' butt flat like two iPhones.' The whole cafeteria was WAAB."

Mr. Wilder and Principal Akers silently looked at each other and shrugged their shoulders, confirming they didn't know what WAAB meant.

Jaylen continued. "And that's when Victor lost it. He shoved Curtis toward me where I was sitting. I caught Curtis, and then I stood up and told Victor to leave them alone. Victor was like, 'You ain't got nothing to do with this, Jaylen. Just get out my way.' I said, 'Yeah, I do. Cause we all be writing in that class. And that shit is real! Ain't nothing cornball about it.' Then he gonna tell me, 'Looks like I'ma have to whip your ass too, then.'"

Mr. Wilder asked, "You weren't scared?"

Jaylen put his fists out in front of himself. "Come on, Mr. Wilder. I tried to told you these hands is vicious. I hit him like three times before he even swung. He tried to grab me, but I ain't let him. If he'd done that, he would've got me."

Mr. Wilder pointed toward DeSean to interrupt. "Where were you during all of this?"

DeSean answered, "Oh, I went looking for security so he could break it up. I found Officer Timmons sleeping in his chair in front of the bathroom again. I had to be real careful how I woke him up too. Cause he had a travel mug full of coffee in his hand."

Principal Akers shamefully closed her eyes and shook her head.

Jaylen resumed. "Yeah, and, apparently, as Officer Timmons made his way through the crowd, those thick, scuba-diving goggles he calls glasses got knocked off his face, and he couldn't see shit. He started grabbing me around my waist from behind. Then he was reaching for Victor's ears and shit. I didn't know what he was doing. But eventually, he grabbed Victor and started taking him to the front office. Twinkie had to give him directions, though. You know, like, 'Turn right. Turn left. Watch your step.' After they left, you know Curtis was talking cash shit."

Principal Akers, butting in a second time, demanded, "Jaylen, please! That vulgar language is unnecessary."

Jaylen asked, "What type of language did you say?"

Principal Akers repeated, "Vulgar."

Jaylen looked over at Mr. Wilder, not knowing what it meant. Mr. Wilder waved him off.

Jaylen was apologetic regardless. "Oh, okay. I'm sorry about that, Ms. Akers. Curtis was talking *major* shit."

Principal Akers looked up at the ceiling and exhaled in frustration.

DeSean raised his voice from the back of the room. "You leaving something out, ain't you, Jaylen? Something about a girl."

Jaylen bashfully smiled. "Oh, yeah. Zoe walked up to me after the fight. At first, she was concerned and asking me if I was all right. I told her I was good. She told me she was glad I did what I did. She said she felt like somebody been needing to put Victor in his place for a while. We talked for a little bit longer, and she told me that she would come up to Burger King on Saturday during my lunch break to eat with me."

Mr. Wilder held back his smile in the presence of an angry Principal Akers. But he discreetly gave Jaylen a thumbs-up when she wasn't looking.

Principal Akers said, "And just so you're aware, Mr. Wilder, Jaylen and Curtis are both now back in in-school suspension. And, speaking of Curtis, where is he?"

Mr. Wilder answered, "His father, Curtis Sr., is not a fan of creative writing. So he decided to pull Curtis out for the time being. I'll be meeting with his father tomorrow, though, to discuss it in further detail."

Principle Akers replied, "Based off what happened today, I'm starting to think that his father might be on to something."

Mr. Wilder cut his eyes at Principal Akers. She asked Mr. Wilder to walk out in the hallway with her. "DeSean and Jaylen, please excuse us for a moment."

Mr. Wilder followed Principal Akers out into the hallway beyond hearing distance from the classroom. She turned around to forcefully tell Mr. Wilder, "Listen, I know that I just gave those boys in-school suspension. But I want you to really drive it home how disappointed you are with them and how this type of behavior will not be tolerated!"

"I understand."

Principal Akers switched the subject. "So what's the status of those guardian papers you told me you would have signed by today?"

"Well, I don't have his mother's signature yet, and for a good reason. But I do have good news."

Principal Akers rolled her eyes. "Go ahead. Tell me what's going on."

"I haven't been able to find her and get her to sign the papers, because at night, she hangs out in some rougher areas where people aren't real big on paperwork."

"Okay, so why don't you ask her during the day sometime?"

"Because DeSean is in school during that time. And I thought it would be better if he were with me, so that she can see that he wants this to take place as well."

"What's the good news?"

"We're going out to find her this afternoon before it gets too late and she's at that bad place I told you about. DeSean is almost 100 percent positive that she will be there and that she will be willing to sign the papers. If everything goes as planned, I will come in first thing in the morning, on my day off, to hand you those papers."

"Okay. Good-night, Mr. Wilder. And good luck." Principal Akers turned to walk away.

Mr. Wilder shouted, "Hey! I know you're already doing a lot for me. But I was wondering if you could do me one more favor?"

Principal Akers stopped to listen.

"It's about your janitor, Jawbone. I met him last week."

"Oh, I didn't know you had the pleasure."

"I wouldn't call it a 'pleasure.' I was thinking more along the lines of misfortune."

Principal Akers's face scrunched up. "What about him?"

"Let's just say that he has a very negative attitude about the creative writing program and, more importantly, the kids who are in it. I don't want them to even have the chance of being influenced by him in some way. I was wondering if you could switch him to the morning shift?"

Principal Akers smiled with a slight giggle. "Come on now, Mr. Wilder. Don't you think that's a bit ridiculous? Some quiet old janitor influencing those boys you have in your class?"

There was a brief silence. Mr. Wilder continued to look her in the eyes without a smile, in pure disagreement. Principal Akers grinned.

"No, Mr. Wilder. I won't be processing the paperwork to switch his shifts. Frankly, I really think you're overestimating the influence of a janitor."

Enraged, Mr. Wilder banged his fist against the locker. He turned to point directly between Principal Akers's eyes. "You listen to me, toots! I don't—"

Principal Akers slapped his hand out of her face. "Who in the hell do you think you're talking to, old man? You do not call me 'toots'! And you most certainly never put your hand in my face again! I am the principal of this school! And that type of language will not be tolerated!"

Principal Akers began to walk away without taking her eyes off Mr. Wilder. "You can come pick up your last check tomorrow...sir!"

Mr. Wilder ran his fingers through his hair and blew out hard. Then, he slowly walked back into the classroom.

DeSean stood beside his desk. Jaylen jumped up to ask, "What's up, Mr. Wilder? Is everything cool?"

Mr. Wilder waved them away as he leaned back through the door frame to watch Principal Akers walk away. "Sit down. Sit down. Everything's fine."

After seeing Principal Akers turn the corner to leave the building, Mr. Wilder walked into the classroom with a smile that stretched clear across his face and displayed his stained, glossy yellow teeth.

"Got dammit! I couldn't be prouder of you guys!" Mr. Wilder walked down the aisle to give Jaylen and DeSean hard high-fives. "That's what the fuck we do! Stick together! Don't let anybody, not a football player, a fucking janitor, or even a bullshit principal change that!"

Mr. Wilder stopped to catch his breath for a moment. He looked at Jaylen and DeSean with excited smiles on their faces. "Holy fuck! I wish Curtis was here! This is what victory feels like, men! Don't you ever let someone tell you that writing isn't competitive! In everything, there is a fucking winner, and there's a loser! Today was a damn-good win! Do you hear me? I said a damn-good win! A great writer will kick your ass and then sit down and write about how he did it!"

Mr. Wilder stopped to look down at his desk and check his notes. "Wow! Today's lesson was supposed to be on being passionate about your writing. What a fucking start, huh? Listen to me, men. You know why there's only two or three of you in this class? Because not everyone has the guts to be a writer—to hear someone slam something you've slaved over for months or to have someone disagree with your opinion. You're a special fucking breed! And don't you forget that! So just write! And let your words flow more from your heart than your mind! Then you keep on writing until your fingers start to bleed! You write until you fall asleep at your desk and wake up with a blood stain on your chair!"

DeSean smiled. Mr. Wilder's comment made him realize where the stain on the chair had come from.

Mr. Wilder finished. "Then, when you're done writing and you've put all your heart and soul into it, you stand by your fucking work with pride! Do you hear me? You straighten your goddamn spine! If you don't have one, get one! And you let your balls hang! If you don't have some, grow some! I don't care how you do it! But you stand by your fucking words proudly! To hell with other people's opinions! If they had enough balls to give a damn, they would write a book themselves!"

—∞—

On that brisk afternoon, DeSean decided to ride along with Mr. Wilder and Jaylen. As the three stood beside the old Chevrolet, DeSean asked

Mr. Wilder, "Where am I supposed to sit with all this stuff you got in the back seat?"

Mr. Wilder unlocked the doors and waved DeSean off. "Ah. Just push that stuff to the side. As skinny as you are, you'll find enough cushion to sit sooner or later."

Through his peripheral vision, Mr. Wilder noticed Jawbone standing in front of the school, holding a mop. He looked directly at Mr. Wilder while shaking his shiny brown head in disappointment. Mr. Wilder told the teenage boys to hurry up and get in the car. While getting in the vehicle himself, Mr. Wilder took the opportunity to stare back at Jawbone and put a stiff middle finger up in the air.

Even though Jaylen's Kool-Aid smile was on his face the entire time, the ride to Burger King was silent. It was obvious to Mr. Wilder that Jaylen didn't feel comfortable expressing himself in the company of DeSean, and vice versa.

To show he was still interested, Mr. Wilder asked, "So what's the big grin about, Jaylen? You're excited about something?"

Putting up a tough front, Jaylen smacked his lips and rolled his eyes. "Nah. Come on, Mr. Wilder. Don't play me like that. I don't get excited no more. That's for kids. I was just smiling about something Zoe said to me earlier."

"My apologies, Jaylen. It wasn't my intention to 'play you.'"

Jaylen smacked his lips again. DeSean giggled.

Mr. Wilder asked, "So do you want to share what Zoe said?"

Before he got out of the car, Jaylen peeked back at DeSean and cleared his throat before speaking nervously. "Nah. Not really. I do have a question, though. What do dudes usually wear on a first date?"

"Traditionally, a guy will wear a collared shirt with nice pants and shoes. But considering that Zoe will be meeting you on your lunch break, I think it would be a good idea for you to wear your work uniform." DeSean used his hands to cover his mouth so he wouldn't laugh out loud.

Jaylen responded, "I knew that. I was just wondering what other guys do." Mr. Wilder looked at Jaylen sideways, silently questioning his last comment.

After Mr. Wilder dropped Jaylen off, DeSean immediately took the opportunity to sit in the front seat. Before his rear end could even make contact with the cushion, DeSean's face appeared to be disgusted. "Why is your apartment so empty, but your car is filled to the brim with junk?"

Mr. Wilder giggled while restarting the engine. "When you walk around all day trying to think of a great story and how to tell it, like I do, you'll tend to be forgetful of people, places, and, yes, even things. I keep all of this 'junk,' as you so eloquently put it, in my car just in case I'm out somewhere and I need something. Now, I don't have to go back home to grab it."

As they approached Tidewater Drive, DeSean coughed out, "Hoarder. Hmm. Hmm."

"Come again?"

"Shorter. Shorter. I was thinking you should make that pile back there shorter so that you can see through your back windshield. Anyway, you're going to want to make this right on Tidewater Drive. Then turn left on Princess Anne. And make another left on Church Street."

Mr. Wilder was so anxious to get the papers signed by DeSean's mother that he ignored DeSean's fearfully inconsistent tone of voice.

They arrived at the corner of Church Street and Brambleton Avenue. Mr. Wilder pulled into the large shopping center. DeSean advised him to park at least ten spaces back, in front of the Family Dollar. Mr. Wilder complied. The car was in park.

Mr. Wilder asked, "How can they call that a memorial for Dr. King? It's just an awkward-looking triangle."

DeSean glanced over his shoulder to peek at the structure again. "Yeah, I know. A lot of people said the same thing. They raised money for years trying to get that thing built. Everybody thought it would be this nice statue of Martin Luther King Jr. But they ended up giving us that. It looks like I could've bought some tile from Lowe's and created it myself."

Mr. Wilder nodded.

DeSean continued. "We need to focus, Mr. Wilder. Look straight ahead, to the right a little." DeSean pointed. "In front of the Save-A-Lot grocery store and then right across the street. You see those people standing over there?"

"Yeah. There's five of them."

"Yeah, those are the other drug addicts she hangs around. They pretty much spend all day trying to get enough money to buy their next hit. My mom is the one with short hair, wearing a shirt and blue jean jacket."

"Okay. But if she's over there, why did you have me park way over here?"

"Because I don't want those other crackheads looking through your car, plottin' to rob you."

Mr. Wilder placed the key in the ignition and started the engine. "I don't have anything in here that would interest a drug addict, trust me."

DeSean rapidly reached to turn off the car and snatch the key out. "Yes, you do. Those crackheads will sell everything you have in here, and the car itself. Crackheads are the best salesmen in the world, trust *me*." DeSean handed the keys back over to Mr. Wilder. "Do you have the papers?"

"Yes, they're in my pocket. Come on, let's just get this over with."

As they walked past the Save-A-Lot grocery store, Mr. Wilder whispered, "Let me do all the talking when we get over there."

DeSean briefly dropped his head and smiled. "If you say so."

Mr. Wilder stood out like a sore thumb among the drug addicts, not only because of his skin color, with everyone else in sight being African American, but also because of his sheer size, evident age, and professional business attire. The two ignored the hostile looks they received. They walked directly toward DeSean's mom.

"Oh, look at this! Mr. Little Goody-Two-Shoes went and fucked up!" DeSean's mother said after being approached by the two.

Mr. Wilder reached out his hand. "Hi, Mrs. Briggs. I'm Mr. Wilder, your son's creative writing teacher."

She waved him off. "Whatever. Look, I don't give a damn who you are or what he did. So both of y'all can get the fuck outta my face as far as I'm concerned. And my name is Patti! You can cut all that Mrs. Briggs bullshit out. His punk-ass father shot me three times just because he saw me suckin' a lil' dick! What the fuck was wrong with him? That shows you how much of a fuck up he was! He was supposed to kill me! At least that's what he said before he pulled the trigger. He couldn't even do that shit right!"

DeSean maintained a stony face throughout their conversation. He appeared to be unaffected by his mother's harsh words.

Mr. Wilder replied, "I think we have a misunderstanding, Patti. Your son hasn't done anything wrong. We came out here to ask if you would allow me to serve as a guardian for DeSean."

"What? Y'all walked all the way over here to ask me that bullshit?" They both nodded. "Where's the papers? I don't give a—"

One of the other addicts nudged Patti on the arm. Patti quickly added, "Oh, and this is going to cost you forty dollars."

DeSean turned his head and blew out hard.

Mr. Wilder explained, "No. I'm not paying you forty dollars to make sure your child has a roof over his head. That doesn't make any sense."

Patti pouted. "I know, but he's my baby, and I love him. That forty dollars is going to help me get through the emotional stress of letting him go." DeSean looked away and shook his head.

Mr. Wilder replied, "Come on! Cut the crap, Ms. Patti! That boy has been homeless and on his own for months now, and you know it! Now, here's the papers. Can you sign them so we can be done?"

Patti straightened up. "Did I tell you that that forty dollars includes a blowjob?"

Mr. Wilder slapped the papers against his thigh. "You're impossible!" DeSean cut his eyes at his mother.

"Boy, don't you look at me like that! If your punk-ass daddy would not have went and killed himself, you would be fine right now, wouldn't you?" DeSean didn't answer. "You got the nerve to look at me all judgmental? I watch your punk ass step over me every morning when I'm laying down in that underpass, like I ain't shit! So don't try to act like you give a fuck about me either. Now, back to you, Mr. Wilkins."

"It's Mr. Wilder."

"I don't give a fuck! Do we have a deal?"

"No, ma'am. We do not have a deal."

Patti rubbed Mr. Wilder's shoulder. "Oh, I know what it is. Y'all old white mothafuckas just want to stick it in my ass. Don't worry, I do that too. Just make it a smooth fifty, and I'll let you do what you want."

Mr. Wilder shoved her hand off him. "What? No!"

"What you afraid of? You ain't got nothing to worry about. My ass is clean! I haven't took a shit in a week!"

"Ms. Patti, I'm not interested in anything except you signing these papers. Can you please do this for you son?"

"Fuck him! He ain't nothin' but a big pussy, just like his daddy."

DeSean's anger reached its limit. He punched his palm aggressively, making a loud slapping sound before walking quickly back to the car.

Mr. Wilder asked one last time, "Will you please sign these papers? Yes or no, Ms. Patti?"

"Forty if you're horny, fifty if you're frisky." She winked one eye.

Mr. Wilder shoved the papers back into his pocket. "Good-bye, Patti."

She shrugged her shoulders. "Your loss."

Mr. Wilder pointed back to DeSean. "No, ma'am. It's his loss!" Mr. Wilder turned to run after DeSean the best he could with his limp and cane.

7

The next day at 5:55 a.m., directly across the street from Norfolk State University's athletic entrance, Mr. Wilder arrived at a newly built brick-front colonial home, with a two-car garage in a gated community. The neighborhood was so quiet, Mr. Wilder heard the birds chirping as he rang the doorbell. His hand hadn't even returned to his side yet before the door was yanked open by Mr. Jordan, a five-foot-eight, muscular, clean-shaven man with short hair and big ears like his son, Curtis Jr. He reached out his thick palm, and Mr. Wilder shook it.

"Mr. Wilder, I presume?"

"Yes, sir. Brett Wilder. Nice to meet you."

"Curtis Sr. Nice to meet you as well. I'm surprised you're early. The artistic type like you usually aren't too big on punctuality."

"Oh, I learned very young that early is on time—"

Mr. Jordan joined in. "—on time is late, and late is not acceptable." Both men laughed.

"I like you already. Was your father military, and you learned that from him?"

"Yes. He served a few years in the army when I was young."

Mr. Jordan nodded. "Good. Well, come on in. We're heading down to the basement. You don't mind talking to me while I do my morning run on the treadmill, do you?"

"Oh, no. Not at all."

Mr. Wilder was in awe not only of the sheer size of Mr. Jordan's man cave, but also the overwhelming amount of authentic sports memorabilia he'd collected on his walls. The treadmill faced a large, muted television that was mounted on the wall. Mr. Jordan hopped on and ran. He read the subtitles to Sports Center while random Motown hits played on the surround-sound speakers.

"Now that we've gotten through the pleasantries, let's get to the meat and potatoes of why you're here. What's wrong, Mr. Wilder?"

Mr. Wilder remained standing. "Okay. You took your son out of my creative writing class. Now, let me say on the same token that I understand why you did it, with him getting in trouble at school and all. But this isn't like taking away a videogame or a cell phone. This is something that I believe your son is really good at, and could possibly earn him a lot of money down the road."

Mr. Jordan didn't even turn away from Sports Center. "I'm going to tell you just like I told Officer Timmons." Mr. Wilder squinted. "That's right. I've spoken to Officer Timmons about my son too. Apparently, my son thinks it's easier to talk to Timmons than me. Because, just like you, all he wants to do is tell Jr. how he can be anything he wants to be and how Jr. should chase after his dreams. Either way, like I was saying, I'm Curtis Sr., and he's Curtis Jr. That means that he's my son. And I will have him do whatever it is that I feel is best for him, even if that means pulling him away from some pipe dream of becoming a great rapper, or writer, or comedian, or whatever the hell he says he wants to be nowadays. Besides, he needs to be focusing on ROTC right now, anyway. That will give him a guaranteed job. He can work hard, save up some money, start a family, and raise them right, just like I did when I married my high-school sweetheart twenty years ago. Now look at us. Look around. This nice house, those nice cars, everybody's looking good and eating good. That don't come from chasing no dead-end dreams. That comes from working hard, doing right with your money, and treating people right."

Mr. Wilder, who'd never taken a seat, even after being offered one, rested his hand on the treadmill to grab Mr. Jordan's attention. They sustained eye contact.

"With all due respect, sir, you're right. He is your son, and with him being seventeen, you are in a position of authority over him. But I must also say that you're right again. About me, this time, though. Because I agree with everything Officer Timmons has said. Mr. Jordan, your son has the unique gift of writing comedy. Let me ask you two questions. I don't want you to answer them. I just want you to think about them. First, what was the purpose of you having a child if you want him to grow up and do all the same things you did? Yes, he can do the plan that you laid out. Or, he could do more. Although I'm very grateful for the military and the protection you all provide us, I believe your son has a gift that can't be contained in a uniform. Second, would you be able to live with yourself knowing that your son will spend the rest of his life blaming you for why he's not living his dream?"

Mr. Jordan stepped off the treadmill. He rubbed his chin to think and then looked up into Mr. Wilder's eyes. "Listen to me. I see your point, but you need to see mine. And the fact that I'm doing what I know will keep that boy off the streets begging for change…or worse…"

"No. I understand your logic fully, Mr. Jordan. You want to guarantee that your son will be a success in life. I get that. But now is the time, and this is the opportunity, for him to chase his dreams. Think about it. If you're right, and he's no good at it, he can still join the military and say that he tried to be a writer. But if you're wrong, he could live the rest of his life making way more money doing what he loves. You really don't have anything to lose by him staying in the program, sir."

Still unsure, Mr. Jordan grit his teeth. "I don't know about all this crap."

"Okay, how about this? Since I see you're still on the fence about it, how about we make a deal?"

"Okay. What do you have in mind?"

"From the music you have playing, I can tell that you like classic R&B. Am I right?"

"Oh, absolutely. I love it."

"Okay. I'll ask you a question about it. If you get it right, Curtis Jr. can't come to my class anymore. If you get it wrong, he can come for the rest of the semester without you pulling him out again."

Mr. Jordan deviously smiled. "Okay, I'm fine with that. I don't think you realize how much I love my oldie-but-goodies. But that's okay. You're going to learn. I wish my wife wasn't asleep so she could hear this."

Suddenly, Mr. Wilder's beeper began to sound. He snatched it off his waistband to see the number. After he saw that it was from the high school, Mr. Wilder wondered, "Why would the school be contacting me so early in the morning...on my day off?" Then he remembered Principal Akers's threat to fire him. Mr. Wilder figured that may have been her trying to tell him that his last check is ready to be picked up.

"Is everything all right? Do you need to use my phone?"

Mr. Wilder shook his head and politely waved him off. He put his beeper back on his waist. "No. No. Everything is fine." Mr. Jordan was the last person Mr. Wilder wanted to inform that he was on the hot seat.

"I have to tell you, I don't think I've seen a beeper in at least a decade now."

"Yeah, I'm not a fan of being accessible twenty-four hours a day. Unlike most people nowadays, I enjoy my alone time. And I don't need a bunch of likes and LOLs to validate myself."

Mr. Jordan smiled and nodded slowly. "So what's the question?"

"Huh? What? Oh, yes, the question. I'm sorry, I lost my train of thought. The question is, Who wrote and sang the original version of the song 'Respect'?" Mr. Wilder nervously bit his bottom lip.

Mr. Jordan's smile grew bigger with confidence. "That's it? You must think I'm an amateur. That's easy. Everybody knows there ain't but one *real* version of that song! And after all these years, the original version is still the best version, written and sung by the original queen diva herself, Ms. Aretha Franklin!"

Mr. Wilder smiled as Mr. Jordan continued to brag. "So, it doesn't look like you'll be seeing much more of Jr. In the meantime, I suggest you start studying soul music before you go around placing bets with people about it."

Mr. Wilder's grin was on full display. He shook Mr. Jordan's hand and patted him on the shoulder twice. "Sir. I need to go respond to the beep I just received. Don't worry, I'll show myself out. But I expect to see Curtis Jr. on time in my class this coming Tuesday." Mr. Wilder walked away.

Mr. Jordan scrunched his face and raced to his cell phone. Mr. Wilder was exiting the house and closing the front door behind himself when Mr. Jordan finished googling the answer. Mr. Wilder heard Mr. Jordan scream from the basement, "Son of a bitch!"

———⚬⚬⚬———

It was seven fifteen in the morning when Mr. Wilder arrived at Booker T. Washington High School. The teachers' parking lot was full. Busloads of students were walking into the building for the school day, which started in fifteen minutes. Mr. Wilder was in no rush to get fired. He allowed all the students to walk in before him. He even held the door open and waited for the stragglers. While walking toward the front office, Mr. Wilder thought, "There's no excuse for what I said. And I can't think of a solution to continue helping the boys when I get fired. Aw, hell, I'll just beg for my job back when the time comes."

Mr. Wilder slowly walked through the doors of the front office with his head down. He looked up and saw Principal Akers standing behind the counter, smiling at him like never before.

As Mr. Wilder approached the opposing side of the counter, Principal Akers graciously asked, "Good morning, Mr. Wilder. Look who decided to pay us a visit this morning?" Principal Akers looked to her right, and Mr. Wilder to his left. What he saw was the backside of a woman wearing black flats, knee-high, skin-tone stockings, and an old gray skirt suit with matching hat and veil clip.

The woman stopped digging in her purse to turn around and look at Mr. Wilder.

"Yes, Ms. Akers! Yes. That's him, Mr. Wilkins! He's the one who was trying to have me make a decision without my Bible in my hand!" The woman held her Bible up in the air. "That's okay! I just got it out my purse! Now we can talk!" Principal Akers continued to smile.

Mr. Wilder rolled his eyes. "Listen. My name is Mr. Wilder. And, Patti, what are you doing here right now?" Patti placed her hand on her chest as if she were offended.

"Excuse me! Are you a member of my church? My name is Mrs. Patrice Briggs, sir. May my late husband rest in peace. Only my brothers and sisters in the Lord call me Patti."

Principal Akers asked, "Oh, what church do you attend, Mrs. Briggs?"

"Oh, I goes to all of 'em, honey. First Baptist, Last Baptist, New Galilee, Old Galilee, Catholics." She paused to do the Holy Trinity. "I even gets down with the Pentecostals too, honey. I just gotta make sure that I wear my tennis shoes to their service. I can't be doing all that running in these flats. They ain't got no ankle support."

Mr. Wilder commented, "So, pretty much, you go to whichever church is serving food to the homeless that day."

Principal Akers slapped him on the wrist.

Patti gasped for air. "Sir! I'm annulled!"

Mr. Wilder smacked his lips. "You're not annulled! You're widowed."

Principal Akers chimed in. "I think what she's trying to say is that she's *appalled* that you would even suggest such a thing."

Mr. Wilder cut his eyes at Principal Akers before gathering himself. "You know what? You're right. I was out of line with that comment, and I apologize. Mrs. Briggs, you came here on your own merit, and I'm thankful for that. So how can I help you?"

Patti smiled. "Now, that's more like it. But don't feel bad, Mr. Wilder. We all fall short of the glory of the Lord."

Mr. Wilder thought, "Yeah, and some fall further than others."

Patti continued. "I'm sure you both know that it even troubles me to say this. But I spent all night praying about it, and I came here today to sign those guardian papers."

Mr. Wilder's eyes popped open in shock.

Principal Akers asked, "Is that right?"

Patti hung her head. "Yes. You know how these kids are today. They're all independent, and they don't need their parents for anything because they have the Internet. I guess my baby DeSean is no different. As much as I want to teach and nurture him, he just has to take his own path."

Mr. Wilder rolled his eyes again while reaching in his pocket for the papers.

Principal Akers rubbed Patti's shoulder. "Oh, I understand, Mrs. Briggs. I can only imagine how hard it must be to watch your son leave your care."

Patti looked up. "Yes. Y'all have no idea how hard this is for me. All I ask for in return is $200 so that I can help provide formula to the babies in the nursery at church."

Mr. Wilder couldn't contain himself. He slammed the papers down on the counter. "What! Yesterday you said fifty dollars! It should be free! We're trying to help your son!"

Principal Akers gently placed her hand on top of Mr. Wilder's. "Wow. What a big heart you have helping these babies in the nursery. Now, Mr. Wilder, calm down. I have no issues with compensating Mrs. Briggs for such a charitable effort." Principal Akers reached under the counter for her purse.

Mr. Wilder said, "You can't be serious right now?"

Patti said, "Thank you, Ms. Akers. I realize everyone at the school is going through tough times right now during this drug investigation. So I didn't want to be too much of a burden."

Still digging through her purse, Principal Akers looked up. "Um. I think you've misspoken again, Mrs. Briggs. They're investigating the murder—"

Mr. Wilder quickly raised one finger in the air. "Wait a minute. Tell us more about this drug investigation."

"Look. I'm sorry if I struck a nerve. But I thought everybody knew that white man killed that little black boy over drugs."

Principal Akers interrupted her. "Now, Mrs. Briggs, I'm going to have to stop you right there. The boy who was killed is named LaVeon Kirkland. And he was a straight-A student at this school. So I highly doubt that he had anything to do with something drug related."

"Oh, I know the boy's name, Ms. Akers. I heard that white man yell it so many times that it's stuck in my memory. And I heard about LaVeon's 'Straight As' too. They didn't come from him doing no whole bunch of studying, either. See, y'all ain't hear this from me. Cause I'm not one to gossip. But I was right here that night when that white man killed that boy. It was almost nine o'clock. I was sitting at the bus stop right beside y'all's football field, straight across the street from Bay Seafood."

Mr. Wilder mentioned, "I wonder what you were doing at a bus stop, alone, at nine o'clock on a weeknight."

Quick witted, Patti replied, "Oh. I was reading my Bible and getting more acquainted with the Lord while I waited for the bus to come and take me to choir rehearsal. Anyway, LaVeon was sitting on the opposite end of the bus stop bench. That white man came running up to him, yelling, 'LaVeon! Why didn't you come to my room?' Apparently, from what I heard, LaVeon had been providing the weed for those lil' parties your teachers like to throw. But he was only dealing with that white man. In return, all of LaVeon's teachers were giving him As. But now, the white man wanted cocaine too. LaVeon told him his boss wouldn't let him do that, and that he'd have to pay. That white man turned red and threatened to turn LaVeon in. LaVeon told him if he got turned in, that he would turn all those teachers in. Then that white man told LaVeon to come back in the school and meet him in his classroom so he could pay him. Y'all know what happened after that."

"Unfortunately, we do. Either way, I have the $200 you requested to help the nursery at church." Principal Akers said. She held the money up in the air. Patti reached for it, but Principal Akers snatched it back. "Not so fast, Mrs. Briggs. You have to sign those papers first."

Patti quickly yanked one of the ink pens out of the flowerpot on the counter and signed the papers. Mr. Wilder stood there, shaking his head in disappointment the entire time. Principal Akers handed Patti the money. Patti folded the money and then stuffed it deep down in her bra with a smile.

"God bless y'all real good!" She busted through the office doors into the hallway, singing, "When praises go up, blessings come down!"

Outraged, Mr. Wilder said assertively, "You should've never given her that money! You know all she's going to do is smoke it up!"

Principal Akers argued, "That's not my problem! As far as I'm concerned, I just put a roof over one of my best students' head and helped a church improve their nursery."

Mr. Wilder dropped his head in his hand.

"Besides, if she hadn't have gotten that money from me, she would've stole it from someone else. You need to understand something, Mr. Wilder. People like Mrs. Briggs have to want to make themselves better. You can't fix them! So let it go! Plus, I like what you're doing for DeSean. He deserves it. And I'm seeing growth."

A mischievous smile came over Mr. Wilder's face. "Thanks for your kind words. But to me, it sounds like you couldn't find a replacement for me, huh, toots?"

Principal Akers pointed directly at his face, almost touching his nose. "Let's get this over with right here and right now! I am Principal Akers to you! Period! And that's regardless of my age or whether candidates are lined up around the corner to teach creative writing part-time to inner-city youths! We will maintain a professional working relationship with each other between these walls of Booker T. Washington High School! If not, I won't go looking for another candidate! I will simply cut your pay and label your position as volunteer! Are we clear on that, Mr. Wilder?"

In shock, Mr. Wilder took a step away from the counter while nodding. "Crystal." "Good."

With slanted eyebrows, Mr. Wilder intensely stared into Principal Akers's eyes. He tapped his fingers on the counter as he spoke politely. "So 'professionally' speaking, could you please remove Jawbone from the afternoon shift?"

Principal Akers maintained eye contact. "If it's that important to you, Mr. Wilder, I am willing to do so."

"Thank you."

"You're welcome. I'm enjoying the tone of this conversation."

Mr. Wilder briefly looked away to roll his eyes. "So do you think there's any truth to what Patti said?"

Principal Akers waved him off. "No way. There wasn't even a trace of drugs found at the crime scene."

"Yes. But it's not hard to steal drugs from a dead person. If LaVeon was a senior making straight As on his own merit, then surely he must've been applying to colleges."

Principal Akers reached beneath the counter and grabbed a manila folder. "I can find that out right now. This is a copy of LaVeon's entire file that I gathered for the police investigation." After looking over a few pages, Principal Akers's jaw dropped as she slammed her index finger on the paper. "Wow. He was a straight-A student for two and a half years with no honors! No college applications, not even a single attempt at the SATs."

"There's our answer." Principal Akers covered her mouth while gasping for air. "Oh my God. This means that I currently have teachers who are doing drugs. I need to call Mayor Newman." Principal Akers sprinted into her office and slammed the door shut.

Mr. Wilder shouted, "And don't forget about Jawbone!"

———⊗∞⊗———

The following Tuesday, at 3:20 p.m., Mr. Wilder hung his head while slowly limping into his classroom bearing his usual attire and supplies.

Jaylen and DeSean sat in their usual seats, waiting. Mr. Wilder noticed Curtis's desk was still empty. He thought, "Mr. Jordan must've reneged on his deal."

Abruptly, Curtis came running past Mr. Wilder. He patted Mr. Wilder on the shoulder along the way. Curtis took his seat.

"A, yo, Mr. Wilder! Why you looking all sad? I thought you'd be happy I'm back."

"I am happy you're back. And it's good to see you. Why were you almost late?"

"Oh, you know, the usual. I was hanging out with Officer Timmons. I was telling him that he needs to stop brushing his dentures like they're regular teeth. That toothpaste be breaking down the glue. He was talking to me a couple of days ago, and they just fell out in the middle of his sentence. He didn't even know they'd fell out, though. I ain't say nothing, either. I just kept staring at them down on the floor, hoping he would get curious about what I was looking at. You know, they say it's rude to interrupt old-ass people when they're talking." Jaylen and DeSean giggled from their seats.

Mr. Wilder responded, "Yes, Curtis. I am a little down today. Because I have to teach you all about the one part of the writing process that I hate. I'm sorry you couldn't have been here last week when I was more enthusiastic."

Jaylen added, "Yeah, Mr. Wilder turned into a straight OG on us last week, Curtis." The three teenagers laughed. Mr. Wilder shook his head in denial.

Curtis spoke up. "A, yo, Mr. Wilder. So what you teaching us about today?"

Mr. Wilder dropped his head and leaned against his desk. "Editors. And in case you're wondering, I know I usually write something on the board. But on this topic, I don't believe it's worth my energy."

Curtis mumbled, "Sounds like I should've waited until next week to come back."

Mr. Wilder resumed. "Men, listen to me. Editors are a necessary evil in the writing process. After you spend a good portion of the year putting everything you have into your manuscript, they come along and tell you how much you suck. The good editors will even tell you why you suck. You pay them to find every little mistake you made and to tell you where your story needs more or less of something. Now, I know it's going to sound like I'm contradicting myself, but they really do mean well. The bottom line is that you have to have thick skin to listen to their recommendations and then go back and incorporate them. Which brings me to my favorite part about editors. *Everything* they say is a recommendation. It is your book. And you must decide, from what they suggest, what you will and will not include. So I don't care who you all pick to be your editors, or even if you all decide not to have an editor at all. I just want you guys to know that next week, your rough drafts should be complete."

Mr. Wilder reached for his cane to help him get off the desk, but he ended up knocking it to the floor. He turned to put his hand on the desk and slowly kneeled to pick it up.

Jaylen hopped out of his chair and picked it up for him. "Here you go, Mr. Wilder." Jaylen handed him his cane.

"Thank you, Jaylen."

"No problem, Mr. Wilder. What happened to your leg, anyway?"

Curtis said, "I bet it's an old football injury, as big as he is." Jaylen took his seat.

Mr. Wilder raised his hand to calm the noise. "No. If I had to call it something, I guess I would call it an old writing injury. My dad was the one who was a big football star in high school. It used to eat him alive that I was bigger than other kids but wasn't interested in sports at all. One day, when I was sixteen years old, my dad brought home this oakwood dresser for my mom. He asked me to help him get it up the stairs. That thing must've weighed a ton. When we were almost at the top of the stairs, it slipped out of my fingers, landed below my knee, and broke my leg. Obviously, I was yelling for help. But my dad kept pushing to get the job done. My mom came and yelled for him to take me to the hospital. His exact words were, 'I'll take him to the hospital as soon as we get this dresser in the room. He doesn't need two good legs to write a fucking book!'"

So my mom helped him get the dresser in the room, and they took me to the hospital. I ended up having a surgery where they were able to fix my leg. But the doctor said if I wanted it to fully function as before, I would have to go to rehab. My father refused to pay for rehab. He said I didn't need full function in my leg because I wasn't an athlete. Again, according to him, all I needed to be able to do was walk, talk, and chew gum if I wasn't playing a sport."

DeSean projected his voice from the back of the classroom. "What did your mom have to say?"

"Oh, she loved the dresser."

The three young men chuckled before DeSean clarified. "I mean, what did your mom have to say about your leg and how your dad handled it?"

Mr. Wilder rashly shrugged a shoulder. "My mom was a huge reader, so, naturally, she supported my writing. But she was so subservient to my dad, she didn't even have a backbone to speak up and tell him when he was wrong. Much less do anything about it."

Jaylen wondered aloud, "So why didn't you just go back and do the rehab on your own once you had a job?"

"I tried. But the doctors told me that the muscle had grown too thick incorrectly to do so. If I wanted full range now, they would have to rebreak my leg and perform surgery, and then I'd have to go through six to eight months of rehab."

Curtis shook his head. "A, yo, Mr. Wilder. That story crazy. But it ain't no way in hell I would've let my dad walk past me with a dresser in his hands! Not while I'm sitting there with a broke leg! I would've tripped him with my good leg, or something."

That evening at Mr. Wilder's apartment, DeSean sat on the floor with his back against the couch. He pounded away at the typewriter. Mr. Wilder opened his bedroom door fully dressed and walked into the kitchen to grab a bottled water from the refrigerator.

DeSean didn't stop pounding the keys to joke, "I'm hearing a lot of keys being pressed back in that room."

Mr. Wilder giggled from the kitchen while looking at the back of DeSean's head. "Yeah, well, every time I pause to think, I'm hearing keys being pressed out here too. I still haven't gotten used to that."

DeSean smiled. "Well, I suggest that you hurry up and get used to it, because you're living with a future best-selling author."

Mr. Wilder grinned and slowly nodded his head. "I'm liking the confidence."

"What are you working on, anyway?"

"I'm writing my first self-help book. It's just a small project I've been thinking about for a little while. Now that I have some time, I decided to do it."

"I guess it's good to switch things up every now and then."

"I guess so."

"That was a deep story you told us in class. Your dad sounds like a mean dude."

"I don't know if I would necessarily call him mean. Racist, stubborn, and willing to go to great lengths to enforce what he believed in seems to sum him up pretty good to me. But I see how that can easily be translated into being considered mean."

DeSean paused from typing to turn around and face Mr. Wilder. "Dang. I didn't know he was a racist too."

"Yep. He sure was. He would drop the N word all the time. But don't worry, the buck stopped there with him. I don't do racism. I refuse to hate other people based off something they can't control. But yeah, my dad spoke freely about his racism too. He always said that the blacks wouldn't be able to accomplish anything after the death of Dr. King. Then, when rap music started taking off, he said that only confirmed it. In his words, 'Rap music is nothing but a bunch of idiots putting down people of their own race. That causes division among the blacks. And everybody knows you divide and conquer. Which means they'll be easy to control again.'"

DeSean thought for a second. "Your dad must be pretty smart to have thought of that way back then. I still believe that's the biggest problem we are having today. Everybody's stuck on doing their own individual things while we continue to lose as a people."

"Yeah, I didn't like my dad's ways, but I have to admit that he had a lot of wisdom."

"Heck yeah. Just think about it. Foreigners own the nail salons and liquor stores we shop at. Most of the NBA and *all* the NFL owners are white. Then, the major record labels are owned by whites. Hell, even the fast-food restaurants they put in the hood are owned by white people. Now, you have all these people making money off blacks. But who are the blacks making money off of?"

"You know, I never looked at it that way, but that's true."

DeSean squinted his eyes a bit at Mr. Wilder's attire. "Hey, Mr. Wilder. Don't you have some clothes that are more…comfortable?"

"What are you trying to say?"

"I mean, I've been living here for a while now. Don't you think it's kind of weird that I've only seen you in that same black suit and sweater?"

Mr. Wilder raised one of his eyebrows toward DeSean. "Um. I apologize if I gave you the wrong impression. But I'm not part of the alternative community, DeSean."

"What? Oh, ew! No! I don't live the alternative lifestyle either! I was just saying—you know, because—aw, never mind."

Mr. Wilder kept his eyebrow raised.

In an attempt to get rid of the awkward stare he was receiving, DeSean changed the subject. "So what's the full story on that bloodstain in the chair? I heard you mention it during class."

"It's pretty simple, actually. I used to write all my books longhand first, and then I would go back and type them. One night, I was determined to finish the longhand version of the novel before I went to sleep. I was using one of those cheap clear plastic pens. I guess I squeezed it too hard, and it cracked. The crack ended up cutting me and making me bleed. I didn't even notice it until the next morning when I woke up. I was so tired when I finished the novel that I ended up falling asleep in that chair. Fortunately, most of the blood got on the chair. The only thing written in blood was my name."

"Wait a minute. I thought you said you were finishing the novel? Your name goes on the first page."

"Yeah, I know. That's a habit of mine. I always wait until the novel is finished before I put my name on it. I guess I'm afraid of someone reading the unfinished product and thinking that it sucks. I want to at least be able to argue that it wasn't mine."

8

The following Tuesday, DeSean banged on Mr. Wilder's bathroom door with a closed fist. "Come on! Hurry up, Mr. Wilder! It's six thirty! School starts in an hour! I still have to shower, brush my teeth, get dressed, and eat breakfast! Why do you always take so long in the bathroom?"

Mr. Wilder's voice sounded even deeper with the door closed. "I'd like to see how fast you'd move at forty-seven years old with a gimp leg in a tight space."

"But why are you even in there getting ready right now? You don't have to be at school until three thirty!"

"Technically, three fifteen. Either way, I know this might sound strange to you, being a teenager and all. But I came from a time where people woke up in the morning, pulled themselves together, and got dressed, regardless of whether they had somewhere to go. They just wanted to look presentable in case somebody decided to stop by. Nowadays, your generation will walk out of the house with pajamas on in the middle of the afternoon."

"But couldn't you let me go first, though, since I have somewhere to go?"

"Of course you can go first—if you wake up earlier and get in here before me. It's not my fault that you get out of bed with just enough time to get everything done before you have to leave. Besides, just because I'm not leaving the apartment doesn't mean I'm not going to work. I do my best writing when you're in school. Now, do you have any more questions? Because the more I talk, the slower I move."

"Nope. I'm good. Please just hurry up, though."

"Don't worry. I will. If *you* talk, I might move a little faster."

DeSean sat on the floor. His head hung with his back pressed against the bathroom door. He begrudgingly asked, "What do you want to talk about, Mr. Wilder?"

"Tell me more about your father. What was he like? What did he do?"

DeSean lifted his head with a hesitant grin. "I know you would expect me to say this about him since he's my father. But in all honesty, I feel like he was the perfect man. Hard working, a good husband, a good father, and, personality-wise, he had this rugged gentleness about him. You know that UGK song I was rapping before we spoke in the showers was his favorite rap song?"

"Really?"

"Yep. I know that's rare for a man who was a journalist for the *Virginian Pilot* for over a decade."

"What! Your dad wrote for the *Pilot* and listened to that?"

"Obviously, that wasn't the only thing he listened to. He was willing to give anything a chance if the artist sounded genuine about his or her lyrics. That's what attracted him to UGK, and his favorite rapper of the duo, Pimp C. But yeah, he listened to them."

"I bet he must've loved Def Leppard too."

"Absolutely!"

"Wow! Well at least that explains how you know how to use a typewriter."

DeSean snickered. "Yeah, my father taught me how. Not verbally, but I just watched him a lot growing up. He would always try to make his articles more dramatic than the story called for. In doing so, he went through reams of paper on a regular basis. So I consistently saw how to operate a typewriter. But that was my dad, Spencer Briggs. He always had to be the best at what he did, no matter the cost. He did teach me a lot of other things too, though, like the importance of education, self-discipline, and money management. Believe it or not, you and him share a lot of the same values."

"Yeah, it sounds like it. Speaking of education, what are your plans for college? You're a smart kid. Have you applied anywhere?"

"Yeah. I applied to ODU and got accepted. I just don't know how I'm going to be able to afford it. The chances of me getting a grant or scholarship at this point is next to impossible. And I don't want to go get into debt with all those student loans."

"I can understand that, but I wouldn't worry about it. Things seem to always work themselves out when you work hard with good intentions."

"Yeah, I hope you're right."

Without warning, Mr. Wilder yanked the bathroom door open. DeSean fell through flat on his back. He looked up at Mr. Wilder, who stood over him. Mr. Wilder was fully dressed in his usual black suit and sweater.

"I'm done. The bathroom is all yours now."

That evening in class, the boys were excited to see Mr. Wilder back to his usual, enthusiastic self. He limped into the classroom at a brisk pace and slapped his business portfolio on the desk. Then, he grabbed a piece of chalk and wrote in big letters across the blackboard, "TEST READERS." He underlined each word twice before tossing the chalk back on the shelf. As usual, Curtis ran into class late. He crashed into his seat, out of breath.

"Let me guess. You were hanging out with Officer Timmons again?"

"Nah. I went looking around the whole school, but I couldn't find him. Then, when I saw it was almost three thirty, I ran here."

Mr. Wilder nodded and then turned to address the entire classroom.

"A couple of weeks ago, I told you guys I don't care how you outline your story, or even if you do it at all, as long as you know how to navigate through the plot. Last week, unfortunately, I had to talk to you about editors and their importance in the writing process. But once again, I said that I didn't care who you chose to be an editor, or even if you wanted to use one at all. With test readers, or 'beta readers,' as some people like to call them, we will be taking a completely different approach. I do have requirements for this phase. And I have them for a reason. The requirements are as follows:

1. Have a survey for the reader to answer.
2. Have a minimum of two readers in your target market and one not in your target market.
3. They cannot be friends of yours.

The reason for these requirements—"

Curtis interrupted him. "A, yo, Mr. Wilder! Can my mama be one?"

Mr. Wilder rolled his eyes. "And here is the recently added number four:

4. No family members."

Curtis smacked his lips. "Dang!"

Mr. Wilder looked at Curtis as he resumed. "As *most* of you can assume, I don't want, and you shouldn't want, anyone to be your test reader who would simply be proud of you for finishing a book. They care about you, and they don't want to hurt your feelings. So their answers will be sugarcoated, if honest at all."

DeSean cleared his throat before asking, from the back of the room, "Why does it matter if they're in our target market or not? People are going to feel about it however they feel about it anyway."

From the front of his desk, Mr. Wilder answered, "That's not true. It's all about improvement. Your target audience is your strength. So your target audience test readers *should* like your book but also give you recommendations for areas of improvement. That one non–target audience test reader will be brutally honest and let you know where you stand to the rest of the world. Those recommendations are usually longer and harsher. But the goal is always to get great reviews from both the target and non-target audience test readers. Then, you know you've written something special."

Jaylen wondered aloud, "So what type of questions should be on the survey?"

Mr. Wilder responded, "That all depends on what type of book you write. I do believe that the last question should always be, 'Do you have any further comments?' Besides that, though, in your case, since you're writing an action-packed novel, you should want to know if the reader could easily visualize the scenes, for starters. Did the reader find any parts to be boring? Then, I would just go on from there. Do you guys understand what I'm saying?"

The three young men nodded their heads. "Okay, I want you all to get your pens and papers out and work on writing your survey questions for the remainder of class."

Everyone complied.

Not much time had passed before Officer Timmons walked into the classroom. He held a saran-wrapped paper plate in his hand containing four pieces of cake. Curtis stood up with a grin as Officer Timmons placed the plate on Mr. Wilder's desk.

"Aw, man. You didn't have to bring all that cake for me, Officer Timmons. It's okay if we can't hang out after school every day. But I accept your apology."

Officer Timmons pointed toward Curtis's desk. "Boy, go sit your simple behind down somewhere." Curtis slowly sat back down.

"All this cake ain't for you. Everybody gets a piece. Now, Mr. Wilder, I'm sorry for interrupting your class. I just wanted to come down and tell you that I think you are a good man, and I appreciate what you're doing with these kids." The two men shook hands.

Officer Timmons then faced the teenagers. "I'm proud of y'all too for seeing this thing all the way through and taking the time to let this man teach y'all something. Y'all keep at it. And if don't nobody else tell y'all, I believe in you. I know you can make whatever dream you have happen."

The room remained quiet for a while. Officer Timmons held everyone's undivided attention. He hesitated to pick up the plate he brought in, and even more so to speak. "This cake is from the party they're having for me down in the cafeteria...for my retirement."

Curtis popped his head up. "What!"

Officer Timmons nodded. "Yeah. This Friday will be my last day."

Curtis buried his head under crossed arms on his desk and immediately began to cry. Officer Timmons looked away at stone-faced Jaylen and DeSean so that he wouldn't start crying along with Curtis.

"Y'all, enjoy this cheesecake my wife made." Jaylen and DeSean nodded. As Officer Timmons sat the plate back down, Mr. Wilder could clearly see that it was a strawberry bunt cake. Mr. Wilder decided not to say anything, though. He knew Officer Timmons's eyesight wasn't the greatest, and he didn't want to interrupt what could possibly be his last words with the boys.

Back at the doorway, Officer Timmons couldn't ignore Curtis's crying any longer. Officer Timmons's eyes began to water, but he wiped them before a tear could fall. He spoke with a cracked voice. "I can't believe this ol' bean head, overbite-having, Mighty Mouse-looking boy over there crying."

His head still down, Curtis replied, while sniffling, "I know you ain't talking. How you have a nappy mustache? You're not supposed to have to comb that. Then your uniform so loose, it fit like a jumpsuit. They got you walking around school looking like a black Barney Fife."

"Boy—"

Mr. Wilder cut off Officer Timmons. "All right. All right. That's enough."

Usually when Officer Timmons and Curtis were cracking jokes on one another, everyone around them laughed. However, that wasn't the case that day. It was obvious to everyone else in the room that that was their way of saying, "I love you, and I'm going to miss you more than words can express."

After wiping his eyes one more time, Officer Timmons used both hands to grab his belt buckle and pull his pants up. His voice was broken as if the tears were only seconds away.

"Now, just because I brought y'all some cake and shit, don't think for one second that I still won't shoot everybody in this motherfucker." Officer Timmons turned around and walked away as fast as he could. The classroom heard the echoes of his weeping from down the hall.

Prior to the class ending, Mr. Wilder reviewed and approved the students' surveys. He was also sure to let the boys know that they had to submit their final manuscripts next class. That was the day before the submissions deadline.

"Failure to do so will result in no consideration given," Mr. Wilder said before he noticed the blank stare on Jaylen's face. "Meaning they won't accept your book late. So everything you've been working on the past few months will go right down the drain."

Jaylen nodded. "Oh, okay."

After class was over, DeSean, Jaylen, and Curtis waited in the hallway while Mr. Wilder locked the classroom door. As he finished, the group began walking down the hallway together. They noticed Principal Akers walking toward them. Mr. Wilder greeted her first. "Good evening, Principal Akers. What are you doing here so late?"

"I know. I was almost home when I realized I left my phone at work. Since I was already here, I was going to come down and see how class was going. But evidently, I'm a little late for that."

Mr. Wilder nodded. "Yeah, it looks like it."

She turned to address the teenagers. "Hey, boys. How was class?"

Simultaneously, they all said, "Good."

After a quick thought, Curtis blurted out, "A, yo, Ms. Akers. Can you be a test reader for my book?"

Knowing what Principal Akers thought about Curtis's rap alone, Mr. Wilder's eyes nervously expanded in anticipation of her response.

Principal Akers's face turned red as she struggled to conjure up a reason to say no. "Um. When would you need to hear back from me?"

"That's the beauty of it. I don't need to hear back from you. I have this survey." Curtis handed the survey to Principal Akers. "It's only eight questions. You answer those and leave it in my locker by the end of school on Friday. Then we straight."

"Ah. That only gives me three nights to read a novel. And I'm pretty busy right now with homecoming and trying to plan my wedding."

Jaylen and DeSean stood behind Curtis. They continued to chuckle as Curtis begged. "Come on, Ms. Akers. Officer Timmons read it in two days with a magnifying glass. So I know you can do it in three. It's only 115 pages. Technically, it's not a novel. It's called a novella."

After a short breath, Principal Akers said, "Okay. I'll do it."

Mr. Wilder's head snapped back in shock. Curtis was so happy that he gave Principal Akers a hug.

Once the lengthy hug came to an end, Curtis handed her a typed version of his book. She held it studiously against her chest.

"Thank you. Can you guys wait for me to grab my cell phone so we can all leave together?"

Mr. Wilder answered, "Sure. That's fine."

Principal Akers had walked away a good bit when Mr. Wilder nudged Curtis. "You can go ahead and scratch that non-target audience test reader off your list."

Outside, the trees were bare. The brown grass lay flat against the ground as evidence of winter nearing. Booker T. Washington High School was decorated inside and out with anything that was maroon, white, and gold in celebration of the homecoming game that coming Friday. That football game would also serve as the last game of the regular season.

Principal Akers had already left, and DeSean decided to walk "home" that day. Curtis's mother was in the process of pulling the car around. Mr. Wilder looked over at Curtis, whose eyes were still pink from rubbing away the tears shed earlier. Mr. Wilder knew that Curtis would put up a hard front if he asked him flat out if he was okay. So he decided to ask both Jaylen and Curtis a lighthearted question and listen for Curtis's tone. The last thing Mr. Wilder wanted was for Curtis to go home and tell his dad that he was upset about something that happened in his creative writing class. He figured now would be the time to ask in case he needed to explain it to Curtis's mother.

"Do either one of you plan on running for homecoming king next year when you all are seniors?"

Before Jaylen could even turn to face Mr. Wilder, Curtis answered with enthusiasm, "Nope! Not me. When you're the homecoming king, that means you have to be tied down to the homecoming queen. I'm not wit' that. I'ma run for homecoming mack! Then, I can have the homecoming queen *and* all her friends whenever I want."

Jaylen busted out in laughter as Curtis got in the SUV to leave. Mr. Wilder shook his head while thinking, "I guess Curtis is okay."

Mr. Wilder waved good-bye to Mrs. Jordan as she pulled away. At his car, Mr. Wilder unlocked the doors for Jaylen to get in first. Mr. Wilder stood there for a bit and looked back at the embellished high school with a smile. He was happy to see that Jawbone was no longer there to stare at him.

With his gimp leg, Mr. Wilder strategically got in the car and started its engine. Unexpectedly, Jaylen slapped his hands together loudly. The sound startled Mr. Wilder, causing him to slam on the brakes.

"I'm sorry about that, Mr. Wilder. But *please* take Princess Anne Road. I know Virginia Beach Boulevard is way quicker, and it puts you off right there, as opposed to Princess Anne Road, where you have to wait at the light and make that awkward U-turn. But that underpass on Virginia Beach Boulevard stank! I think somebody ran over a skunk under there."

"Okay. Calm down, Jaylen. I'll take Princess Anne. Besides, that gives us more time to talk, anyway."

Jaylen rolled his eyes and slammed his head against the window.

"Give me a break. Don't try to act like you don't like talking to me. I guess the first date with Zoe went so well that you don't need any advice on the second one, huh?"

Jaylen's frown instantly became a smile. He sat back up in the passenger seat. "Nah. Actually, I've been meaning to talk to you about that. The first date went good. Matter fact, the first date went so good we became boyfriend and girlfriend. Then she asked me to go to home-coming with her."

"That's all good stuff. It sounds like you know what you're doing. What do you need to talk to me about?"

"No. That's not all good. I don't know how to dance."

"You definitely came to the wrong person about that one, Jaylen. I'm not even an amateur in that department."

"I figured as much. But couldn't I keep her entertained all night with good conversation and laughs?"

"I'm sure you could if you were on another date. But seeing as you're going to be at a dance, that's what people go there to do—dance and let loose." Mr. Wilder put his car in park in front of Burger King. "If I were you, I would try to find someone who *can* dance, and ask that person to give you a crash course on the basics."

"Yeah, I think that's a good idea, Mr. Wilder. I don't want to be that awkward, stiff dude at the party."

9

The next morning, after a valiant effort to wake up early enough to beat Mr. Wilder to the bathroom, DeSean still encountered a locked restroom door. He tugged on the knob a bit. Its sound grabbed Mr. Wilder's attention.

"Hey! Good morning, DeSean!" Mr. Wilder shouted through the door.

DeSean was still frustrated from having to wait to take a shower. Now, added to that was the possibility of being subjected to more of Mr. Wilder's questions—questions that may as well have been asked by Darth Vader, from the obscure echo that came from the bathroom. DeSean blew out hard through his nostrils and reluctantly answered.

"Good morning! Do you mind if I watch a little TV while I wait?"

"Sure. Go ahead. I think those batteries should still work in there."

DeSean walked over to the kitchen bar where the TV sat. He pressed the small switch at the bottom to the "on" position, and nothing happened. DeSean flipped the television over to check its batteries.

Mr. Wilder wondered aloud, "Should I be expecting you in late Friday night? Or maybe even early Saturday morning?"

DeSean was so distracted from the leaking battery acid he'd found in the TV that he was unable to focus on Mr. Wilder's question. He rushed to the sink to wash the remainder of the acid off his hands. "What's going on Friday night?"

"Homecoming!"

With the batteries now removed, DeSean slid the battery cap back on the television. He unwrapped its cord to plug it into the nearby socket. "No, I don't get involved with that crap!"

"Why not?"

The television displayed a black-and-white static screen. DeSean turned the volume completely down to avoid its pestering sound. "That's just not my thing! Believe it or not, I prefer being alone. Besides, who would I go with? What would I wear? And who would I speak to while I'm there? I don't have a girlfriend. And nobody speaks to me at school. Yeah, Jaylen and Curtis will be there. But they will be wrapped up with their dates. Plus, everyone there will have new clothes and a fresh cut. I would be wearing my same ol' clothes with my same ol' dried-out afro-puff ponytail. I'm not going out like that. I already know what they think about me. I don't need to make myself subject to those awkward situations and potential jokes."

DeSean paused to listen, but Mr. Wilder had no response.

"What's wrong with this TV? All I'm getting is static!"

"You have to play with the antennas. Make sure it's on channel three. It will clear up."

DeSean turned the volume up a little so that he could hear when the static cleared up. Not being able to get the antennas into a perfect position, DeSean feverishly smacked the side of the TV. Instantly, the local news appeared in clear black-and-white. Mr. Wilder slowly walked out of the bathroom in his usual attire. He quickly raised one hand in the air while rushing to stand behind DeSean.

"Whoa! Easy does it."

DeSean rolled his eyes and glanced back at Mr. Wilder, thinking, "Apparently not."

The sun had risen by that point in the day. Its light shined through the window and reflected off the handheld-size TV, which caused the two to use their hands to block the glare.

A middle-aged, Hispanic female reporter said, "Good morning, George. I'm currently standing on Virginia Beach Boulevard, directly behind Booker T. Washington High School, where I can tell you the smell is awful. Parents, students, teaching staff, and even nearby residents have been filing complaints about the stench coming from the underpass for the past week. Just moments ago, workers found and removed the dead body of a woman named Patrice Briggs. I apologize. We do not have a picture to put on the screen at this time. First responders cannot confirm, but they do believe the cause of death is a drug overdose."

DeSean dropped his head. He stood there, watching in his shorts and T-shirt, with a towel thrown across his left shoulder. Mr. Wilder, who still stood behind him, saw a tear fall down his face. He raised his right hand to place it on DeSean's shoulder. But after hesitating, Mr. Wilder decided not to. The reporter continued.

"This is not the only news surrounding Booker T. Washington High School as of late. As you all may recall, last night was the hearing of

Riley Schmidt, a thirty-three-year-old Caucasian English teacher here at the school on trial for the murder of his student, LaVeon Kirkland. The seventeen-year-old African-American male with a 4.0 grade point average was fatally shot here at the school during nonbusiness hours. Mr. Schmidt was found innocent of all charges after claiming self-defense. This is Sophia Munoz of channel—"

Mr. Wilder reached around DeSean to turn off the television. DeSean continued to sniffle with tears effortlessly flowing down his face.

"I know what you're thinking, Mr. Wilder. Why is this boy crying over his crackhead mother? He should be happy he doesn't have to worry about her embarrassing him anymore."

Mr. Wilder silently shook his head. "No."

"She was all I had! Before there was you! Before there was Jaylen! Before there was Curtis! She was all I had! My only family! My only everything! Even though she made my dad so mad that he killed himself and tried to kill her, even though she was on drugs and embarrassed me, and even though she hated me because I reminded her of my dad, I still loved her! You don't know how fuckin' hard it was for me to step over her every goddamn morning underneath that underpass! She'd be laying there surrounded by used condoms and empty needles. Shit, sometimes the needle would still be stuck in her arm. I've even seen mornings where I thought she was dead my damn self! But still, every morning, I would kick all that bullshit away from her and even pull a needle out of her arm if I had to. Then, I'd grab her jacket and toss it over her shoulders to make sure she stayed warm and got rest. Because I knew she needed it."

DeSean sat on the couch and grabbed one of the pillows to cover his face as he wept. He didn't care to see Mr. Wilder standing there, staring at him in his moment of weakness. Abruptly, Mr. Wilder snapped his fingers and rushed to his bedroom. Seconds later, he came out with a hand-carved tobacco pipe.

"Sit up, and scoot over." Mr. Wilder took a seat on the opposite end of the couch. "And for God's sake, take that pillow off your face."

DeSean slowly complied as he looked over at Mr. Wilder. The white of his eyes had turned pink beneath the flood of tears that continued to race down his cheeks with every blink. Even though it hadn't been packed with tobacco, Mr. Wilder gently placed the ebony-stained pipe above his bottom lip. He bit down hard while staring back at DeSean.

"What's up with the pipe?"

"Whenever my dad sat down to tell me a story, he always had this pipe in his mouth. I don't know what it is about it, but every time he told me a story, it stuck with me. Of course, he'd be smoking it. But it was the 70s. Everybody was smoking everywhere back then. Right now, I'm about to tell you a story that I believe you should hear. I grabbed the pipe hoping that what I'm about to say sticks with you."

DeSean rejected with one hand slightly raised. "Oh, nah. Come on, man. I don't need some sob story to help me feel—"

Mr. Wilder cut him off by beginning. "*My* mother passed one month after I was married. She was the most consistent, positive presence

I had in my life. She loved me for being me, just as I was, regardless of whether I played a sport or not—even at the expense of disagreeing with my father one time and getting slapped around because of it. I'll never forget the way I felt that day when I got the news that she'd passed from heart failure in her sleep. Even though I had my wife and my stepson, I'd never felt more alone. The only biological family I had left was my dad, who I hadn't spoken to since I left home for college. It was then that I realized that I would have to learn how to open up to other people, mainly my wife. Although I thought our marriage was pretty good at the time, we became a lot closer when I decided to open up and tell her all my thoughts and feelings. My point is, I know you feel alone right now in this big world. But you're not. You should step out of your comfort zone and open up to a few people. Make a genuine friend who you can share things with. Yeah, you might get hurt along the way, or maybe even further down the road. But that's called living. If you stay in your own safe little bubble, you'll end up watching everyone else around you living their lives while you're just waiting to die."

DeSean used his forearms to wipe away the fallen tears and then turned his lips sideways. "I don't know. I'll think about it."

Mr. Wilder reclined on the couch. "Fair enough."

"But wait a minute. If you hated your dad so much, why do you have his pipe?"

"That's the second point of my story. I snuck in my parents' room and stole this pipe off my dad's dresser when I left to go to college. Now, I'm not saying what I did was right. And I certainly don't want you to start going around stealing. But what I am saying is that this pipe is symbolic of the only good memories I have of my dad. He was a great storyteller. That's what I prefer to focus on. I suggest you do the same in regards to your mother. Focus on the positives, no matter how long ago they may have been. Take those, and save them as precious memories."

DeSean nodded silently. He decided not to go to school and stayed at home with Mr. Wilder so that he could grieve in private.

The next morning, Mr. Wilder stayed in his room long enough to allow DeSean to use the bathroom before him. Once he heard the shower water running and the sporadic splashes from DeSean bathing, Mr. Wilder walked out of his room fully dressed. Mr. Wilder could hear DeSean begin to recite rap lyrics again while showering. He shook his head in disgust before tiptoeing out of the apartment, softly closing the door behind himself.

Mr. Wilder drove to the high school. Initially, he wasn't able to turn into the parking lot as usual. Protesters of various age groups (mostly high schoolers) surrounded the parking lot in mass quantity. He put on his turn signal, but no one stopped to allow him in. Mr. Wilder became impatiently frustrated and inched the car forward while blowing the horn. Feisty protesters greeted him by slapping the hood of his car, screaming, "This is a protest! Turn around!" "Respect the movement!" and "Find somewhere else to park!" He was forced to stop.

Mr. Wilder was in the process of putting the car in reverse when he looked up and saw Jaylen and Curtis removing people from the hood of his car. They eventually created a path for him to enter.

Mr. Wilder pulled into a spot and cut his car off. He noticed the small number of cars in the parking lot. The largely African American crowd, dressed in all black, could be heard chanting, "Arrest Mr. Schmidt!" The demonstrators continued to lap the parking lot while carrying home-made banners displaying statements that varied from "LaVeon was my homie!" to "Black Lives Matter!" to "We ain't going to take this shit!" and every other disgruntled phrase imaginable.

By the time Mr. Wilder got out of his car, Jaylen and Curtis had nearly circled the parking lot. Now they were in front of the main entrance doors. Mr. Wilder waved for them to stop as he limped toward them with his cane. They complied. With his hands down, Jaylen held a "Black Lives Matter" sign by its wooden handle at his waist. Mr. Wilder looked them both in the eyes before glancing down at the sign, and then back up at Jaylen's eyes.

"'Black Lives Matter,' huh?"

"Damn right," Jaylen said with his chest out while staring back into Mr. Wilder's eyes. Not wanting to cause a scene among the other pro-testers, Mr. Wilder clenched his fist by his side.

Curtis asked, "A, yo, Mr. Wilder. What you doing out here? We all out of signs, but you can still march."

"No. I'm not interested in that in the least bit. Can you two come inside with me so we can talk?"

Curtis answered, "Okay." He and Mr. Wilder took a few steps to-ward the school.

Jaylen argued, "I'm not stepping foot in that school until I see some justice."

Now enraged, but careful not to start an uproar among the antsy crowd, Mr. Wilder turned around with both fists balled at his sides, hastily gimped back to Jaylen, and whispered in his ear, "Don't try to play that hard-core tough-guy bullshit with me. Have I ever told you anything wrong?"

Mr. Wilder could feel Jaylen's face shake. "No."

"That's what I thought. Now, since you've realized that I don't tell you anything wrong, I'm telling you to get your ass in that school, because there is some shit you need to hear." Jaylen stood there for a moment to collect his thoughts, and then he caught up with Mr. Wilder and Curtis at the doorway.

The trio sped through the empty hallway on their way to the main office. They were greeted by Principal Akers. She stood behind the front counter in a skirt suit, prepared for business as usual. But nothing of the sort seemed to have been taking place.

Principal Akers frowned. "Mr. Wilder? What are you doing here on your day off?"

"Don't you worry, I'll get to that later. Right now, is it okay for Jaylen and Curtis to wait for me in your office?" She agreed and lifted the countertop for the boys to walk through. Once her office doors were closed, Mr. Wilder stood toe-to-toe with Principal Akers. He pointed toward the entrance doors of the school.

"Why are you allowing that crap to take place in front of the school?"

She was taken aback. "What? Allowing! Really? I'm not allowing anything. That's a peaceful protest going on outside, and they have every right to be out there doing it. Trust me. I checked with Mayor Newman. There's nothing that I can do about it."

"Peaceful my ass. You should've seen what they did to the hood of my car."

Principal Akers brushed him off. "Mr. Wilder, I've seen your car. I doubt they could've made it much worse."

He gritted his teeth. "Where's Officer Timmons when you need him?"

"Even though tomorrow is officially his last day, he called out sick. How ironic is it that just about every teacher on my staff called out sick today too?"

"They're all afraid of the protesters."

"I know. The only teacher who came in today was Coach Bucky. But that's just because he wanted to shine the helmets for the homecoming game tomorrow night. Besides, all the blacks love him because he's the head football coach."

Mr. Wilder rolled his eyes and shook his head. "I need to go talk to these boys. When I come back, you and I need to discuss a couple of things."

"Okay. I'll be here."

Jaylen and Curtis stood side-by-side as Mr. Wilder busted into the office, forcefully closing the door behind himself. He stood toe-to-toe with the teenage boys.

"What the hell are you all doing taking part in that unorganized Black Lives Matter bullshit? Fuck Black Lives Matter! Fuck White Lives

Matter! Fuck Blue Lives Matter! Fuck the KKK! And fuck every other group of dumbasses who think that only their lives matter! That's horseshit! Listen to me, and get this through your heads. *All* lives fucking matter! And until you two and every other dipstick in this godforsaken country can realize that, *all* people will continue to die! And how dare you two, of all people, say that 'black lives matter'? Does my life not matter to you? Huh? Jaylen, do you think you would've had a girlfriend right now had you said that shit you told me you were going to say? And, Curtis, your ass would be in ROTC right now had I not went and talked to your dad. But my life doesn't fucking matter!"

Curtis explained, "Your life does matter. Black Lives Matter doesn't mean that your life doesn't matter. It's just what the movement is called."

"Horseshit! I've never read a romance novel titled *How to Kill a Bitch*! So why would a 'movement' be called something it doesn't stand by?"

Jaylen shouted, "Man, you don't understand us! Being black, all we got is each other! Now these white racist motherfuckas want to take that away from us too!"

Mr. Wilder's piercing eyes stared directly into Jaylen's. He yelled back, "Well, what the fuck do you want, Jaylen? Huh? Tell me exactly what it is that you want!"

"I want white people to stop killing black people and getting away with it."

"Oh, that's just great. Hey, listen, since we're in dreamland, how about I ask for a unicorn to run past my apartment and drop off a winning lottery ticket at my front door? What I'm saying is that's unrealistic. What you just asked for is the result of something. It's not just going to happen because you asked for it. That's like saying I want muscles. They don't just appear. You have to work out for an extended period of time. Now, I see that you're angry, and I can understand why. But you all are going about it the wrong way. Seriously, think about it. If the POTUS were to fly down here right now, open up the door of his airplane, and ask, 'What do you all want?' what would be said? And who would say it? Do you all even have a definite leader?"

Curtis answered, "Shit, I'll say it."

Mr. Wilder turned to face him. "Oh, you're prepared to be the leader, huh? You'd be willing to lay out a plan, negotiate requests with high-ranking officials, and give speeches to the Black Lives Matter 'movement'? And let's not forget that you have to lead by example too. So you're also willing to get spit on without retaliating, sprayed without retaliating, gassed without retaliating, beaten with a billy stick without retaliating, and sometimes even arrested and thrown in jail for no reason…without retaliating?"

Curtis mumbled, "Hell naw. Hell naw. If a motherfucka spit on me, I gotta swing. I'll be nonviolent after."

"That's what the last great African American leader, Dr. King, had to endure."

Jaylen disagreed. "Man, fuck all that nonviolent shit! For me, it's an eye for an eye at this point."

Mr. Wilder calmly asked, "Okay, Jaylen. Instead of me arguing back and forth with you, let me ask you something. Do you think the 'eye for an eye' approach is smart, being that you're the minority?" Mr. Wilder paused. He and Curtis looked toward Jaylen for an answer. After not hearing a response, Mr. Wilder resumed. "That's what I thought. 'An eye for an eye' means that you would lose. So once you all decide as a group whether you're going to be nonviolent—"

Curtis interrupted him. "Whoa! We've been nonviolent!"

"Nonviolent my ass! Damn near every protest that group of yours has ends in a fucking riot! Learn a lesson from the Black Panthers!" Curtis was silenced. "If you truly want to do something effective, you should draft amendments to these laws that allow people to walk free after murdering! Then, have them implemented at every level, from local to federal! Y'all love to rave about the civil rights movement, but look at what they did. They were organized, they had a definite leader, everyone involved agreed to be nonviolent, and they had specific requests. That's how you get things done."

Jaylen complained, "Ain't nobody tryin' to do all that political crap. All them politicians say the same thing: 'We want to bring attention to the issue.' That just mean we want to tell everybody about what's going on, but we ain't gonna do shit about it!"

Mr. Wilder countered, "If they're not doing what you asked them to do, then you make them do it! Don't think of the civil rights movement as just a bunch of black people doing sit-ins, marches, and getting physically abused. One of the biggest game changers was when they decided to boycott the buses. When the blacks decided to walk, versus paying to ride, the transportation business started losing money at an alarming rate. And I can tell you right now, a guaranteed way to get people's attention is by messing with their money."

Curtis mentioned, "But don't nobody be riding the buses like that for real no more."

"Okay. But there *are* other businesses. And what about making sure that everyone who's eligible votes?" Both teens looked shocked. "Yes. That's right. You can vote for more than just a black president, you know. I'm talking from the small local positions all the way up. Listen to their campaigns and vote for the people who you believe would help to enforce a fair law enforcement and judicial system. Write to the current leaders, and let them know that their positions are in jeopardy if justice isn't served. Blacks aren't the minority in this city. Your requests will be heard and taken seriously. But first, you all have to make them. All these riots and acts of violence will only get you thrown in jail, which creates two major problems. One, you will have a record that will affect you every time you attempt to do something professionally. And two, you lose your right to vote when you're incarcerated."

Jaylen and Curtis looked at each other and nodded silently. They turned to face Mr. Wilder.

Jaylen said, "Okay. I can get with that," as he handed his "Black Lives Matter" poster over to Mr. Wilder.

"Good. Now, Curtis, can you dance?" Curtis scrunched his face, wondering why Mr. Wilder asked him that. "Yeah. Why?"

"Good. Teach Jaylen how to dance."

In unison, they shouted, "Oh, hell naw!" and walked as far away from each other as they could.

Curtis continued. "I'm not 'bout to rub my ass on another dude!" Jaylen shook his head and buried it in his palm.

Mr. Wilder explained, "No! Not like that, Curtis! Jaylen is going to the homecoming dance with his girlfriend, Zoe, and he needs to know how to dance with her."

Jaylen took another look at Curtis and said, "Fuck that. I'll learn on YouTube. Besides, I'm not taking another piece of advice from Curtis after what happened the last time. I almost died."

"What happened?" Mr. Wilder asked curiously.

"I was telling Curtis about Zoe, and he asked if we'd kissed yet. I was like, 'Nah. Why?' He said, 'When you do, you need to make sure that you put a Jolly Rancher in your mouth so your breath don't stink.' I was like, 'Cool. That makes sense'...till she put her tongue in my mouth and knocked the Jolly Rancher down my throat. I was out there choking, trying to cough it up. My eyes got all watery and shit."

Curtis raised an eyebrow. "You must've been using the grape-flavored Jolly Rancher. I told you to stick with strawberry. Cause that don't be happening when I do it."

Mr. Wilder argued, "Jaylen, that's nonsense. The dance is tomorrow night, and you can't practice with YouTube, or your mother, because I'm sure she'll be at work. So it's now or never."

Grudgingly, Jaylen shook his head. "Okay. I guess so. Come on, Curtis."

As he walked toward Jaylen, Curtis said, "Okay. I'll teach you how to dance, but Mr. Wilder, you have to close the blinds in this office. I have a reputation to keep."

Mr. Wilder sighed and then reached to pull a loose wire that shut the blinds. When Mr. Wilder turned around, he saw Jaylen and Curtis standing directly in front of each other. "Come on. Get on with it, you two. This shouldn't take all day."

Curtis leaned in to grab Jaylen and then stopped to complain. "A, yo, Mr. Wilder. I can't do this. I'm used to grabbing the girl's ass when I dance."

"Bullshit! You grab my ass if you want to. I bet you that will be the last fuckin' thing you'll ever grab!"

"See, Mr. Wilder? I can't work under these conditions."

Mr. Wilder reeled them back in. "All right. That's enough of that. Curtis, put your hand on his lower back." The two assumed the position before Curtis stopped again.

"Man, what's wrong with your back?"

Jaylen lifted his shirt and removed a large box of condoms from his waistband. He placed them on the desk. "My bad. I forgot I had these."

"How the hell you forget you had that big-ass box? And what you plan on doing with thirty-six condoms and one wee-wee, anyway?"

"Curtis, shut up! My mom gave me those this morning for home-coming night. She said she didn't want me having sex at all. But if I'm going to do it, I need to be safe so I don't end up a teen parent like her."

"Okay. But why you got to bring the whole box, though? Just put one or two in your wallet. Where in the hell would you put that big-ass box, anyway? A girl couldn't even dance with you on a slow song! Your ass would be over there just clunkin' with every step! Now you got to lie about it 'cause you don't want her to know you got a medicine cabinet full of rubbers waitin' on her ass in yo' back pocket! Talking 'bout, *'I don't know what that sound is. This song must be the remixed version!'*"

Mr. Wilder intervened. "Okay. Cut it out. Curtis, the condoms are on the desk now. Let's get to the dancing, please."

The young men returned to their positions and began to dance. Once Jaylen started to get the hang of it, he looked down at Curtis and smiled.

Curtis's eyes bulged. "Hey, man! This ain't romantic, now! Just because I'm teaching you how to dance don't mean you can look in my eyes, smiling and shit. Look over there!" Curtis pointed.

After a while, amid constant bickering between the two adolescents, Mr. Wilder watched Jaylen develop as a dancer. The three walked out of Principal Akers's office and stood behind the front office counter. They waited for Principal Akers to get off the phone.

Principal Akers removed the phone from her ear, used her hand to cover the mouthpiece, and turned around to face the group. "Here, this is for you, Jaylen. It's your mother. Apparently, she doesn't know about you protesting today."

Jaylen smacked his lips and rolled his eyes. He grabbed the phone from Principal Akers and took a few steps away from the group.

While Jaylen was on the phone, Principal Akers's face lit up with excitement. She placed her hand on Curtis's shoulder. "Oh, I forgot to mention that I read your book, Curtis! I really enjoyed it! I've never read a book that made me laugh so hard! I never would've known you had that in you. Very well written. Oh, and I filled out the survey, but I forgot to bring it in. Is it okay if I bring it to you tomorrow?"

Mr. Wilder's face displayed shock at Principal Akers's review.

Curtis answered, "Oh, I'm done protesting. I've decided to take a different approach. So yeah, I'll be in school tomorrow. You can give it to me then. Thank you, Ms. Akers."

"Oh, no, the pleasure was all mine."

After gently placing the telephone back on the hook, Jaylen walked over to join everyone.

"Is everything all right with your mother?" Mr. Wilder asked.

Curtis commented, "Well, whatever it is, we know she's not pregnant. That's for sure."

"Curtis, I'm telling you! You better leave me alone!"

"A, yo, my bad, Jaylen. I couldn't help myself. My bad."

Jaylen took a deep breath to calm down. "She was just telling me that my dad texted her and said that he would come to the writing competition."

Curtis and Mr. Wilder silently nodded. Principal Akers spoke up.

"That sounds like good news. Aren't you excited?"

"Nah. Not really, Ms. Akers. I've learned not to get my hopes up too much anymore. My dad's known for canceling at the last minute."

"Oh, I'm sorry. I didn't know."

"That's okay. Mr. Wilder, can you give me a ride home?"

Curtis butted in. "Oh yeah, I'ma need a ride home too, Mr. Wilder!"

"Yeah. Sure. You guys just have a seat over there on the couch. Principal Akers and I need to have a discussion in her office first. That's what I drove up here for."

In Principal Akers's office, with the door shut and blinds closed, Principal Akers sat behind her desk. "What's on your mind, Mr. Wilder?"

Mr. Wilder stood across the desk, thrusting his cane in the air. "Don't give me that horseshit! You know what's on my mind! Patti died from a drug overdose! And that shit is your fault, not mine!"

"Excuse me! Have a seat, Mr. Wilder!"

"I don't feel like sitting!"

"If you don't want me to stop your pay and cancel this entire writing program right now, I suggest you sit!"

Mr. Wilder blew out hard and flopped down in the chair. Once seated, he stabbed his cane on the ground as Principal Akers continued.

"Thank you. And let's not forget our agreement of professional dialogue with one another. Now, to answer your question, yes, I did hear the news of Patrice's passing. And her death was neither my fault nor yours. She did what she wanted to do with that money. I realize you have more years of life than me. But let me tell you something I've learned growing up in Detroit and living here, where these things happen all the time. Had we not paid her that money, eventually it would've been DeSean found dead in that underpass. You're doing the right thing by helping DeSean. You just have to remember that death is a part of life. Some people play the hands they were dealt, and they see it all the way through until the end. Others decide to throw their hands in early."

Mr. Wilder looked at the floor as he sat there, switching his cane back and forth between his hands.

"How's DeSean taking it?"

Mr. Wilder looked up into her eyes. "Harder than I would've expected. But he'll be fine."

"Are you sure? I know a good counselor."

"Oh, no! That boy's been through enough, don't you think? The last thing he needs is somebody fucking with his brain. Just give him some time. He'll come back around. That's one of the things I've learned with *my* years of experience." Principal Akers frowned her lips. "Whatever happened with those other eight teachers?"

"I thought I'd be able to find proof of them giving LaVeon false grades. So I went back and checked his tests, quizzes, and even his graded homework. But I couldn't find anything. They were all perfect scores. Then, I conducted a 'random' drug test and made sure I included all those teachers. But once again, I couldn't find anything."

"Yeah, I figured as much. It's been over a month, so it's all out of their systems."

"Regardless, I still made a list of the eight teachers' names and submitted them to the police department to be included in the investigation. The officer told me that without proof of drug use or proof of forged grades, it would be very difficult to build a case against those teachers."

Mr. Wilder smacked his lips. Principal Akers resumed.

"I know. I wish I could do more too. But even as the principal, I can't fire those teachers without justifiable cause. Let's face it. With exception to those eight teachers who aren't going to say anything, you and I are the only two people who know that this murder was drug related. But we have no way to prove it."

"No, we don't. But even if we could prove it, that doesn't mean that he should've killed that boy."

Principal Akers nodded.

Mr. Wilder dropped off Jaylen and Curtis. He returned to his apartment to find DeSean sitting on the floor against the couch, typing.

"So you decided to take another day to grieve, huh?"

DeSean stopped typing to look up. "Oh, hey, Mr. Wilder. No, that's not the case at all. I was planning on going to school today. But when I saw what was going on in the parking lot, I decided to stay home. I didn't want to get caught up in all that mess."

"You're not a fan of Black Lives Matter?"

DeSean shrugged his shoulders. "To me, it's not about whether I'm a fan of them. I'm my own person. I agree with some of the things they do, and some of it, I don't. Don't get me wrong. I know racism exists. But I just feel like if I treat people right and do right, everything else will take care of itself. I mean, there are a few stupid people in every race. But I don't think it's right to walk around treating the majority like they're one of the few stupids."

"I understand. And I see you decided to stay here and write instead."

"Yeah. The book is really pretty much done. I just had a few final edits I had to make."

Mr. Wilder nodded and began walking toward the kitchen.

DeSean picked up the stack of papers next to him on the floor and stood up. "Hey wait!" Mr. Wilder stopped. "I wanted to know if you would be one of my test readers?"

Mr. Wilder gently pushed the stack of papers away. "I don't know about that, DeSean."

"Why not? You meet both the requirements. You're obviously not my family. And you've made it more than clear that you're not my friend." DeSean extended the papers again.

Mr. Wilder accepted them. "Okay. Fine."

DeSean grinned. "Thanks, Mr. Wilder. I can't wait to hear what you think. Oh, and I wanted you to know that I gave a lot of thought to what you told me yesterday morning. And I think you're right. I do need to step out of my bubble. I'm still not going to the homecoming dance, though. But I will go to the homecoming game."

Mr. Wilder raised an eyebrow. "Well, I'm glad that you listened to me and, more importantly, that you decided to open up to people. But don't you think it's a little soon for that, with your mother's passing yesterday?"

"Yeah, but life goes on, right? I can't continue to sit here and sulk over it. Besides, the way I see it, I lost my mother months ago when she started using drugs. What I lost yesterday was the hope of my mother coming back."

10

The Tuesday morning after homecoming, Mr. Wilder sat on the couch with his legs crossed, waiting for DeSean to get out of the bathroom. Mr. Wilder had already showered and dressed long before DeSean had awoken. After Mr. Wilder heard the shower stop running, he went and stood with his back to the bathroom door. Mr. Wilder impatiently held a sheet of paper in his hands. After what seemed like a lifetime to Mr. Wilder, the bathroom door slowly opened.

DeSean, in only his undergarments, said, "*Mr. Wilder?*"

Without turning around to face DeSean, Mr. Wilder extended the sheet of paper above his head. "I read your book. Before I tell you what I think about it, I'd like to know the title. I only see your name on the cover page."

Never stepping forward to make eye contact, DeSean continued to look at the back of Mr. Wilder's balding head with a smile. "When you told me you wrote all those books and they didn't get published, I decided to do the exact opposite. So I wrote my name first and waited to put the title last."

Mr. Wilder didn't find DeSean's comment to be humorous. He sighed.

"Okay. I wanted you to read it first before I put a title on it. I couldn't decide on one. But I'm leaning toward *Mr. Wilder*. What do you think?"

"I think that fits naturally, considering he's your protagonist. I loved the story. A middle-aged white man helps three troubled male adolescents navigate their way through the struggles of urban society. You didn't veer too far away from the truth, either, did you? You definitely have your father's journalism blood running through you."

DeSean simpered.

"I'm guessing I'm supposed to be Mr. Wilder, huh?"

DeSean nodded. "Yes."

"Okay. I like it. It's a great story, and it's very well written. This caliber of book just might win the competition."

DeSean leaned forward to show Mr. Wilder his oversized grin.

Later that afternoon, Mr. Wilder arrived at Booker T. Washington High School, excited to collect Jaylen's and Curtis's manuscripts for submission. He walked into the classroom with DeSean's manuscript cuffed in his palm, pressing against his side. Mr. Wilder was stopped in his tracks by DeSean, Jaylen, and Curtis, who stood only steps away from the classroom door. They wore homemade costumes.

DeSean put his hand up. "Excuse me, sir. With today being our final class before the competition, we've decided to surprise you with Writers Jeopardy!" DeSean extended his arm toward the blackboard. It was decorated with Jeopardy-style categories: "Sci-fi Novelists," "Romance Novelists," "Horror/Suspense Novelists," "Drama Novelists," and "Action Novelists." Mr. Wilder glanced over at the board and then back at DeSean, who had a black sock that he'd taped on hanging from his chin.

"And who are you supposed to be?"

DeSean answered, "Well, to get you warmed up, here's the clue: despite dropping out of school to work when my dad was sent to prison, I managed to write classic pieces of literature that stood the test of time, such as *A Christmas Carol* and *David Copperfield*."

Mr. Wilder immediately said, with a smirk, "Charles Dickens."

Jaylen was up next. "All right, sir. If you could, please place the manuscript you're holding over there with the rest of them, and have a seat anywhere you'd like in the students' desks."

Mr. Wilder complied. Once Mr. Wilder was seated, Jaylen said, "I was a school teacher before I became a sailor. And——"

Mr. Wilder interrupted him after looking up at the black sock Jaylen had taped across his face like a beard. "Herman Melville!"

Jaylen dipped his head. "Dang. I couldn't even finish the question." Mr. Wilder chuckled.

Mr. Wilder had a comfortable smile on his face as Curtis approached. He wore a brown blazer over his school clothes. "A, yo, Mr. Wilder. I wanted to be Ernest Hemingway, but we ran out of socks... and I'm black. Anyway, long before Martin Luther King Jr. ever had a dream, I'd written novels that many literary critics say helped change race relations."

Mr. Wilder snapped his fingers and briefly looked up at the ceiling to think. "Oh. Richard Wright!"

Curtis silently nodded as he backed away to stand next to Jaylen and DeSean. With a full-blown smile and his legs crossed, Mr. Wilder slapped his hand down on his desk in arrogance. "I would say I'm warmed up now. So which one of you am I playing against?"

The three teens turned to face one another as Principal Akers came rushing into the classroom. She had a plate full of homemade chocolate-chip cookies in her hand. The clicking sound of her high-heeled shoes echoed with each step.

Jaylen pointed. "She's your competition. We're the game hosts."

Mr. Wilder raised an eyebrow. "All right."

After she placed the cookies on the teacher's desk, Principal Akers said, "So it looks like you've made it through the warm-up questions, Mr. Wilder. I just wanted you to know how great of a job you've done thus far here at Booker T. Washington High School and how glad we are to have you as our creative writing teacher. Now, boys, even though we all worked together to do this for Mr. Wilder, you all should be proud of your accomplishments as well. Regardless of what happens at that competition in a few weeks, each one of you can say that you've written a book. And that's no easy task.

"All right, let me get off my soap box and back to the man of the hour. So for your final warm-up question, can you tell me who I'm supposed to be, Mr. Wilder?"

He sat up in his chair to listen.

"I wrote a series of books that were so popular—"

Without blinking, Mr. Wilder shouted, "J.K. Rowling!"

"No! Come on, Mr. Wilder. You can't tell from the glasses and the dark wig? I'm supposed to be E.L. James."

Curtis blurted out, "Freak!" Everyone laughed as Principal Akers shook her head with a grin. "Okay, let's get started."

Nearly an hour had passed, and the game was tied with one question left. DeSean found himself asking all the questions while the other two so-called hosts watched and ate chocolate-chip cookies. The category was "Sci-fi Novelists" for five hundred.

DeSean read the description. "Despite my family telling me, 'Honey...Negroes can't be writers,' I went on to win multiple Hugo and Nebula awards. I originally began writing to avoid being bullied. And even though my mother wanted me to be a secretary, I think I've made her proud."

Mr. Wilder slapped his hand down on the desk to answer first. "Um. The only black sci-fi novelist I know is Samuel Delany. So who is Samuel Delany?"

"I'm sorry, but that's incorrect, Mr. Wilder," DeSean said.

Jaylen and Curtis got hyped up. "Uh oh! Ms. Akers 'bout to get you, Mr. Wilder!"

DeSean looked at Principal Akers. "You can win right now if you get this right. If not, we'll have to declare this game a tie."

Principal Akers fearfully bit her lip. "I must admit, I'm not much better than Mr. Wilder in this category. I only know of one black sci-fi writer as well. Who is Octavia Butler?"

"Wow. You're right."

Jaylen's jaw nearly hit the floor. "Dang! I can't believe you lost, Mr. Wilder."

Curtis started running around the room shouting, "Oh snap! She said Octavia's maid used to write sci-fi!"

Mr. Wilder remained seated while shaking his head with a smile on his face. He shook Principal Akers's hand. "Congratulations. Great job. That was a lot of fun."

"Yes, I agree. I enjoy a good, friendly competition every now and again."

Soon after, there was a moment when everyone was about to leave the room, and yet there was silence. Everyone looked around at one another, not wanting to leave. It was as if a mutual bond of care and understanding had just been solidified. Although never said, each person seemed to have the words "I love you" resting on the tips of their tongues.

⸻ ❧ ⸻

A few weeks passed, and it was time for the awards ceremony. Earlier in the week, Mr. Wilder took the time to clean out his car. He wanted to ensure that Jaylen, DeSean, and Curtis arrived on time and sat together. Although they arrived early, Mr. Wilder was forced to park across the street, next to the fire station. The Scope's parking garage had already reached full occupancy.

Once out of the car, the chill of the mid-December night put a pep in everyone's step as they walked toward the red carpet. Mr. Wilder and Jaylen trailed behind DeSean and Curtis by a few steps on the sidewalk. That morning, in anticipation of winning the competition, DeSean decided to spend some of the money he'd saved on his appearance. After getting a haircut, DeSean walked to a local thrift store. There, he bought brown leather boat shoes, tan khaki pants, a bright multi-colored plaid shirt, and a black tie. Curtis wore a royal-blue suit and matching shoes with an all-black shirt and tie set. Walking beside each other, they looked like a Mexican drug lord and a southern Baptist preacher.

Still more than arm's length behind the two, Jaylen's loose-fitting khakis, striped dress shirt, and Timberland boots made him look like an extra in a 90s R&B music video. Mr. Wilder walked alongside him, having only added a tie to his otherwise-predictable attire.

Jaylen glanced over at Mr. Wilder. He spoke in a low tone, careful not to be overheard by DeSean or Curtis. "My mom told me my dad ain't coming."

"What! I'm sorry to hear that. Are you okay?"

"Oh, yeah, I'm fine. I was actually expecting him to cancel this time. I'm learning not to get my hopes up anymore when it comes to him."

Mr. Wilder pursed. "When did you find this out?"

"Earlier today when I was at work. Fortunately, sometimes on Saturdays I can work an eight-hour shift. So I was able to stay busy and not give much thought to it." Mr. Wilder nodded.

They approached the red carpet entrance designated for writers who'd submitted work for the competition. The crowd of fans surrounding the red carpet varied in age from teenagers to senior citizens. Among them were news reporters and photographers hassling writers for interviews and pictures.

The crowd, dressed in sleek, modern clothing, frowned at the three teens. Although no words were said, the young men could feel the disdain of the onlookers. With not one interview requested or one picture taken, Jaylen, DeSean, and Curtis were rushed down the carpet by an impatient photographer.

"Come on! Hurry along! Hurry along!"

Curtis complained, "Damn. We can't even get a picture?"

Jaylen added, "Yeah. I already see how this shit 'bout to go tonight."

Mr. Wilder yelled, "Hey! They're with me!" The sound of his cane tapping the concrete beneath the carpet became rapid as he caught up. The students had gotten ahead of him when they noticed the spotlight on the red carpet and raced toward it.

When the crowd saw Mr. Wilder's face, there was an immediate applause. The recently judgmental group of people began shouting over one another.

"We love you, Vegas!"

"I've read all of your books!"

"Can I have a picture with you?"

The once impatient photographer begged Mr. Wilder for a picture. "Vegas! Sir, could you please stop for a pose?"

"Fuck off," Mr. Wilder answered as he continued down the carpet alongside his students, who bore confused expressions.

"Who the hell is Vegas?" DeSean questioned as the group reached the door.

Mr. Wilder shook his head and ignored him while reaching for the door handle. Before he could grab it, the door opened from the inside. The group backed away from the door as an elderly Caucasian man with a thick white beard walked out in a black tuxedo.

"Vegas! Old Buddy! How are you?" the man asked with a smile while holding a cigarette between his fingers.

Mr. Wilder proudly shook his hand. "Theodore! Sir, it's good to see you. I've been doing well. How about yourself?"

Jaylen, DeSean, and Curtis were thrown off by Theodore's English accent. They'd never heard anything like that before. They were even more thrown off by Mr. Wilder's unusually giddy demeanor.

"Splendid! I was just stepping out for a few puffs before the presentations begin. Do you care to join me?"

"Oh, no, sir. I gave up smoking a while back."

DeSean cleared his throat to speak. "Excuse me, sir. Why do you keep calling him Vegas?"

Jaylen and Curtis nodded as Mr. Wilder dropped his head.

"Ah, yes. You see, he and I have known each other for the better part of fifteen years. Before I retired, I was the publicist for his first published novel, which was published by Summit's Creek at this very competition and went on to be his first best seller. Since then, he's submitted a novel every year, totaling four best sellers, and has a record nine competition victories. His other six novels went on to achieve success in the self-published realm."

DeSean thought, "Mr. Wilder told me those fifteen books were never published. And I bet that's why he retired from the chicken company too. It wasn't because of some boring-ass stock investments."

Theodore saw Curtis roll his eyes and sigh. "Ah. I'm terribly sorry. Do please forgive me for my rambling on. You see, young man, people in this industry don't receive nicknames without just cause. The trouble with Vegas is that no one knows him personally. Even I, myself, who's known him for quite some time, has no knowledge of his personal life—where he lives, where he works, if he works, family? Not even the foggiest. I'm sure you all are familiar with the adage 'What happens in Vegas, stays in Vegas'? That's how he received the nickname. Every year he shows up with his book, and we don't see or hear anything from him until it's time to do it again the following year."

Mr. Wilder chuckled before Theodore asked, "That begs the question, how do you all know Vegas?"

Jaylen answered, "Oh. He's our tea—"

"Host!" Mr. Wilder interrupted. "I'm their host. I met this group of young writers in the library one day and convinced them to submit their work in the competition."

The boys squinted at Mr. Wilder. Curtis mumbled under his breath, "I ain't ever been to the library."

Theodore raised an eyebrow and curiously stared at the group of four. "Very well. Good luck, gentlemen. And a good evening to you all."

Behind the entry door was a long hallway—a foyer of sorts that bore small metal lockers along its walls from floor to ceiling. There was a large yellow sign that hung above the door straight ahead: "No Cell Phones Allowed In Theater!"

Mr. Wilder looked over at the young men. DeSean said, "I don't have a cell phone."

Jaylen commented, "Yeah. Me either."

Curtis looked away and then smacked his lips. "Dang, man! I just got my cell phone back yesterday when I got off punishment!" Mr. Wilder didn't care. He pointed toward the lockers.

With Curtis's phone in a locker, the group walked down the well-lit hallway and through the metal door into the theater. They stopped for a moment to allow their eyes to adjust to the dim lighting atop the crowded stadium seating. The air was filled with subtle chatter and faint classical music. On stage, there were black curtains draped down to the wooden floors. In front of the curtains, the projector screen had been pulled down. It displayed a slideshow of great novelists, such as Toni Morrison, Edgar Allen Poe, John Grisham, James Patterson, John Steinbeck, Mark Twain, Danielle Steel, Margaret Atwood, Harper Lee, Zadie Smith, and Langston Hughes. Off to the side was a cherrywood podium with the words "Summit's Creek Publishing House" engraved on it.

Standing at the middle rear of the theater, Mr. Wilder noticed Curtis Sr. in the far-right walkway. He stood there repetitively glancing at his watch. Mr. Wilder ducked his head in hopes of not being approached again and led his students over to where Curtis Sr. stood, which was twelve rows away from the stage.

Jaylen and Curtis trailed behind while DeSean pestered him. "I didn't know you had a nickname."

"Well, now you do. It's just something they started calling me, and it stuck. You heard the story."

"Yeah, I did. But why didn't you want to tell him that you're our teacher?"

"Because he was right. I like to keep my personal life personal. I've told you that before."

DeSean had more questions. But he knew he'd lost Mr. Wilder's attention as they approached Curtis Sr.

Next to Curtis Sr.'s empty end seat was his wife, Mrs. Jordan, and then Jaylen's mother, Ms. Tonya, and Jaylen's girlfriend, Zoe. There were four empty seats in the row behind them that Curtis Sr. had saved. Jaylen sat behind Zoe, DeSean sat behind Ms. Tonya, and Curtis sat behind his mother after walking past his dad with an attitude.

"Hello."

Curtis Sr. replied to his son with an argumentative, "Hello!"

Mr. Wilder had the chair at the end, behind Curtis Sr. Before taking his seat, though, Mr. Wilder was introduced to Zoe. She was a thin teenage girl with golden-brown skin, long curly jet-black hair, and braces.

Jaylen had to jog her memory. "He's the white dude I was telling you about."

Mr. Wilder just sighed and looked at Jaylen from the corner of his eye.

Mr. Wilder also gave Ms. Tonya and Mrs. Jordan hugs.

Ms. Tonya complained, "Look now, Mr. Wilder. I don't mean no disrespect to nobody or nothing like that. But Jaylen better when this money—I mean, competition. I done took time off work and paid for a babysitter just to be here."

"Well, I can tell you that he's written a great book, Ms. Tonya. But as you can see from the crowd in here, the competition is thick. I think he has a chance, and his book is certainly worthy of it. But ultimately, it's going to come down to the judges."

Finally, Mr. Wilder took a step back and into the aisle, where he shook Curtis Sr.'s hand. Curtis Sr. stood there watching the other six become more acquainted. Mr. Wilder faced Curtis Sr. at an angle, being sure to remain discrete by keeping his back to the crowd.

"Hey, Curtis, thanks for saving those seats for us."

"Oh, no problem. I wouldn't be caught dead in here if it wasn't for y'all. So I figured we may as well sit together."

Mr. Wilder rolled his eyes and sighed as Curtis Sr. continued. "Y'all made good time too. This thing is supposed to start in three minutes— and it better! The sooner Jr. gets this pipedream out of his system, the better off he'll be. Matter of fact, I got his ROTC uniform in the trunk of my car right now."

Mr. Wilder had had enough. "All right. I'm going to take my seat now. It was good talking to you, Curtis."

"Hey, wait a minute. How did you know that about Otis Redding?"

Mr. Wilder looked him in the eye. "My mother had a huge crush on Otis Redding when I was a kid. She kept it a secret from my dad, though."

"Yeah, I see why. A white woman having a crush on a black man back in those days wasn't acceptable."

Mr. Wilder briefly squinted at Curtis Sr. and then grinned subtly. "Yes, that's true."

On the way to his seat, Mr. Wilder recognized an old friend by the back of his head. As soon as Mr. Wilder's bottom touched the seat cushion, he heard DeSean's foot tapping on the concrete floor below. DeSean immediately sat up to see past Curtis and address Mr. Wilder.

"I still have some questions I need to ask you!"

Mr. Wilder put his right hand up. "Okay. Calm down. You can ask me after the presentations tonight. They're about to start in a minute and it'll only last an hour. Relax."

DeSean crossed his arms and blew out hard, slamming his back into the chair.

Mr. Wilder adjusted his blazer and nudged Curtis with his forearm. "Hey, come with me. I have an old friend of mine I want you to meet." Mr. Wilder ducked his head and led Curtis five rows closer to the front, where an old man in a black suit with a small, gray afro sat. Mr. Wilder tapped the man's shoulder.

"Hey, buddy. How are you?" When the man turned to look up at Mr. Wilder, Curtis saw his face and ran toward him.

"Officer Timmons!" Curtis wrapped his arms around Officer Timmons's chest and rested his head on his shoulders, in true bear-hug fashion. Officer Timmons squeezed back. With his head still on Officer Timmons's shoulder, Curtis opened his eyes and saw his father watching him from four rows back. Curtis Sr.'s lips were tight with jealousy. Curtis let Officer Timmons go.

"Man, I missed you, Officer Timmons. But what you doing with that long black undertaker suit on? This ain't no funeral."

Officer Timmons smiled. "I missed you too, Curtis. I didn't miss that bright-blue suit you have on, though. Your skinny ass walking around here looking like a strand of Christmas lights."

Mr. Wilder looked up at the ceiling. "Oh boy. Here we go."

Officer Timmons's wife nudged his leg.

"Nah. We don't have time for all that right now. Maybe after the show. Y'all, this is my wife right here." Officer Timmons faced his wife. "Baby, this is Curtis and Mr. Whitey. I mean Wilder. Mr. Wilder."

She was a classic, mature woman with radiant skin and long curly salt-and-pepper hair. Her flawless smile was on display as the two shook her hand.

"Curtis, I'm always telling my wife about how hard you've been working on this. So I wanted to make sure that we were here tonight to support you. I want to let you know that no matter what happens tonight, I wouldn't have missed this for the world."

Curtis's eyes started to water. He gave Officer Timmons another hug.

"A, yo, thanks, Officer Timmons. That means a lot." Curtis let go and used the back of his index finger to wipe the moisture from his eyes. "I'ma go sit down now."

Through his peripheral vision, Mr. Wilder could see the host walking across the stage toward the podium.

"Yeah, maybe I should be heading back to my seat now too."

Officer Timmons whispered, "Hey, hold on! Don't think for one second that I didn't notice how you was looking at my wife. I know she's fine. But she's all mine. Y'all white boys be wanting you a little scoop of chocolate ice cream every now and then, don't you? Not over here...not over here."

Mr. Wilder shook his head. "No. I wasn't thinking anything of the sort, Officer Timmons."

"Uh huh. Come here. Let me tell you something." Mr. Wilder took a step forward.

Officer Timmons grabbed his arm and pulled it in close to his body. Mr. Wilder's forearm was pressed against Officer Timmons's hip.

"You feel that right there? That ain't one of my many muscles, neither, boy. That's right. They let me keep my service pistol. So if shit gets crazy in here tonight, all you got to do is say the word. I'll shoot everybody in this motherfucker." Officer Timmons let Mr. Wilder's arm go. Both men adjusted their suit jackets.

"I don't think that will be necessary. But thanks for letting me know that, Officer Timmons. I'm going to go take my seat now."

The thin, naturally redheaded woman in a black-and-beige night-gown spoke.

"Good evening, ladies and gentlemen, and welcome to the seventeenth-annual Summit's Creek Publishing House Grand Writer Awards ceremony—" the audience applauded—"or, as we employees of Summit's Creek like to call it, 'The Greatest Hour of Writing.' My name is Samantha Bach, and I will be your hostess for the evening.

"Tonight, there will be four awards given, totaling $60,000 each." The audience applauded. "First will be the adolescents, who will each receive a $40,000 scholarship to any college of his or her choosing and a $20,000 publishing contract with Summit's Creek. There will be one winner for the best nonfiction book and one winner for the best fiction novel. From there, we will move over to the adults, whose winners will each receive a $60,000 publishing contract with Summit's Creek." The audience applauded again. "And just like the teenagers, the adults will have one winner for the best nonfiction book and one winner for the best fiction novel.

"Now, for the one house rule. As you all can see, many have traveled from all across the Commonwealth of Virginia to be here. Whether you've submitted a book, you're supporting someone who's submitted a book, or you're in the Summit's Creek Avid Readers Academy, like me, and you've been buried in submissions for the last month, we can all appreciate the hard work that goes into these literary pieces. So please, no booing if you disagree with any of the decisions made here on stage tonight. Thank you, and, as always, can we have a round of applause for the owner of Summit's Creek Publishing House and the man who made all of this possible, Mr. Jack Summit?"The audience applauded again.

Mr. Summit stuck his head out from behind the stage curtains with a large smile and waved to the crowd. After Mr. Summit went back behind the curtain, the hostess continued. "Now, without further ado, here are the nominees for best nonfiction adolescents."

The projection screen showed each author's name and the title of his or her book as each nominee was called. In between the announcements, the screen resumed the generic Summit's Creek symbol. The winner for that group was a small teenage Hispanic boy for his book entitled *Coping with Parents Who Live Vicariously Through You*. As he stood up on the opposite side of the theater to go accept his award, his parents stood as well. They adjusted the young man's tie, blazer, and hair. When he got to the podium, he invited his parents on stage to stand with him. Then, he pulled out an index card from his suit jacket and began to read. The first sentence of his acceptance speech was, "I'd like to start off by thanking my parents for helping me organize my thoughts for this book." His parents stood behind him with enormous smiles of pride.

Once he finished, the hostess returned to the podium. "And now, for the award in fiction for adolescents. This year, we have three action-packed finalists. And the nominees are: Charlie Steinz for the novel *Sin City Ransom*. We all know who to call when bad things happen. But who do we call when an entire city is held hostage? In Las Vegas, where large amounts of money flow like a river, the leader of the country's largest bike gang surrounds the desert-bound city demanding specific items, which include insane amounts of money for him and his gang-sters. Until his requests are met, he has vowed to blow up one luxuri-ous hotel every hour, on the hour. No matter the outcome, blood will be shed. And if not by the gang members, by the city's lead officials." The audience applauded.

"Next, we have Jaylen Edwards for the novel *Bloodline Warriors*. At a time of modern warfare, a foreign country has built a wall on its perim-eter. Anyone who tries to enter or fly over it has been shot and killed. In a desperate attempt to infiltrate the wall and gather information, the president personally enlists the two greatest warriors to ever wear a US uniform. They just happen to be a father and son who haven't spoken in years. While getting reacquainted, they must rely on each other's strengths to complete the mission. Will they be able to forgive each other and move past their differences? Or will carrying their emotions on the battlefield prove to be too much of a war in itself?"The audience applauded again.

"Our third nominee for this category is Kang JiYeon for her novel, *The War of Oceans*. In the year 2500, the world as we know it has been flooded for the past three years. There are two boats full of survivors—one in the Atlantic and one in the Pacific. The survivors have been aim-lessly floating and living off the sea, each group not knowing of the other's existence. One day, land emerges, and both boats arrive on the shore. Will the two be able to reside peacefully with each other? Or will people repeat the actions of the 'old world,' and make the 'new world' subject to the effects of war?" The audience applauded.

Samantha ripped open the envelope. "And the winner is Jaylen Edwards for his debut novel, *Bloodline Warriors*!"

During the applause and excitement, Curtis told Jaylen congratulations before he sat back down and dropped his head in disappointment. Jaylen gave his mother and Zoe each a hug and kiss on the cheek. Jaylen then scooted down the aisle and shook Mr. Wilder's hand with a feeling of gratitude on his way to the stage. As he walked, Ms. Tonya shouted, while jumping in front of her seat, "That's my baby! That's my baby!"

At the podium, the applause came to an end as everyone stood. Jaylen looked down at the front row and observed an excited Principal Akers, who continued to applaud for him.

Jaylen waved while speaking into the microphone. "Hey, Principal Akers. I didn't know you would be here."

As Principal Akers waved back, Jaylen noticed her presumable fiancé next to her. He was a tall, lean man with a well-trimmed beard and tailored suit. He squeamishly remained seated.

"Dad?" Jaylen said. The room fell to complete silence.

Principal Akers faced the man. "Dad?"

Jaylen asked, "What are you doing here? You told me you couldn't make it!"

The guy stood up and buttoned his suit jacket to explain. "Listen. I've told you I'm an entrepreneur. My schedule changes a lot. So I can't guarantee I'll be anywhere. But I'm here now. Congratulations son."

Principle Akers continued to face the man. "Son?"

Ms. Tonya wanted to leave her row and go to the front, but she was being held back by Mr. Wilder. Ms. Tonya screamed from her seat, "You ain't no entrepreneur! You a entrepa-whore!"

Jaylen agreed. "Yeah, man. Don't feed me that entrepreneur bullshit. Do you know how much crap my mom had to go through just to be here tonight? But obviously, going on a date with your fiancé is more important to you. So yeah, Ms. Akers, that's my dad, Justin Leonard."

Principal Akers gasped. "I can't believe you're Jaylen's dad! We were about to get married, and you never even told me you had a child!"

"I don't need to tell you I have a child! As you can see, the boy is doing fine! And you would've never known I had a child had you not begged me to come here with you and sit in the front row. Plus, what do you mean 'were' about to get married?"

"Wow. It means that the wedding is off. And you and I are so through! I refuse to be with someone who won't even acknowledge his own child." Principal Akers held her left hand in the air. "Oh, and I'm keeping this ring. I think that's only fair considering the amount of time I've wasted with you."

Jaylen said, "Damn. It looks like you fucked up everything, Justin."

Justin pointed up toward Jaylen. "Boy, I don't know who in the hell you think you're talking to! But you better watch your damn mouth! I'm still your father!"

Jaylen snatched the microphone out of its holder and marched to the edge of the stage, directly in front of Justin. "What! Mr. Wilder, cover your ears please!" Jaylen stared deep into his father's eyes. "Nigger, my mama more of a man than you are! You've never been shit, ain't shit, and will never be shit to me, Justin!"

The crowd murmured. Justin was in the process of taking his jacket off to run on stage when he was approached by two bulging men who towered over him. Both gentlemen unbuttoned their suit jackets as one of them said, "Sir. We think it's best that you leave now. Right this way please."

Justin argued, "I ain't going no damn where! I paid to be here just like everybody else!"

Both gentlemen snatched Justin's arms and pulled him close to their bodies. The man who'd spoken calmly repeated himself before they walked. "I said right this way, please."

The crowd applauded at the action that had taken place. As the clapping came to an end, Jaylen stepped back behind the podium and gave a brief acceptance speech.

"First of all, I'm sorry that y'all had to see that. Secondly, I'd like to thank all the people who made this possible. My mom, Mr. Wilder, Zoe, and even Curtis and DeSean. Everybody in here knows how hard it is to finish a book. But knowing that y'all two were going through it with me helped me get past a lot of those tough parts. Finally, I'd like to thank Summit's Creek for choosing me. In all honesty, I've never really thought about college. And that $20,000 is nice to have, but I really don't know what I'm going to do with that, either. That's a lot of money. But I can promise y'all this: I will do everything in my power to not be anything like that guy who was just escorted out of here! Thanks again, and y'all have a good night."

The crowd rose for a standing ovation as Jaylen left the stage.

11

Jaylen returned to his seat. Curtis Sr. stood to button his suit jacket. "Junior, listen. Your mother and I are about to leave. Now, you can stay here and see what happens with your friend, or you can come with us. It's up to you. But I hope you can see how much of a waste of time this was, chasing after some pipe dream. What do I always tell you? Go for the guaranteed paycheck, manage your money right, and then you can do whatever you want *over time*. You weren't even a finalist! And I expect to see you in that ROTC uniform come Monday. Do you understand me?"

Curtis sat silently with tears trickling down his face. He looked up into his father's eyes. "Yes, sir."

DeSean wrapped his arms around Curtis. Jaylen leaned in, shoulder-to-shoulder with the two.

Curtis Sr. turned and extended his hand out to Mr. Wilder, who stood to shake it.

"I kept my word, Mr. Wilder. Are we good?"

"Yes, you did. And yes, Mr. Jordan, we're good."

Curtis Sr. waved for Mrs. Jordan to follow along before Samantha, the hostess, rushed to the microphone.

"Excuse me, everyone! I do apologize for the delay. But in what has already been an unforgettable evening, we are about to do something that has never been done in the seventeen-year history of this competition."

Curtis Sr. stopped in his tracks and raised an eyebrow.

"Backstage, just now, Mr. Jack Summit himself has decided to offer a $40,000 scholarship in exchange for the publishing rights to *The Adventures of Loose Butt*, a comedic novel written by Mr. Curtis Jordan. Mr. Jordan, please come down to the stage to accept your award."

The crowd gave a round of applause. Curtis jumped out of his seat with a smile. He wiped the tears from his face and gave Jaylen and DeSean high fives.

"Let me put my hater blockers on," Curtis said before putting on a pair of shades he'd pulled out of his suit jacket. He scooted out of the row and slowly walked past his father. Curtis Sr.'s jaw rested on the floor in disbelief.

"Excuse me, Pops."

His mother, Mrs. Jordan, grabbed his arm and yanked him in for a suffocating hug that left one side of his face covered in makeup and lipstick. "I love you so much, Son. And I'm so proud of you. I knew you could do it," she cried.

"Thanks, mama. I know. And I love you too." Curtis straightened his suit jacket, and headed back down the aisle, where Officer Timmons shook his hand and patted him on the back. Mr. Wilder stood, leaning against the wall, waiting for Curtis.

"What are you doing, Mr. Wilder?"

"Following you on stage."

"Why? You ain't do that to Jaylen."

"Yes, but I'm afraid of what *you* might say." Curtis smacked his lips.

Curtis demanded attention by waving to the crowd on his way to the stage. Mr. Wilder trailed behind, raising his suit collar and ducking his head beneath it.

The hostess spoke over the stimulated crowd. "I'm so excited to be able to present this award to Mr. Jordan. I personally read this hilarious novel and could not stop laughing. It has instantly become a favorite among the Summit's Creek Avid Readers Academy. The hardest thing to do was compare it to the traditional novels, which is why it wasn't a finalist. This laugh-out-loud story details the struggles of a fifty-seven-year-old Asian stripper called Loose Butt as he attempts to turn his life around by becoming a Christian rapper. Now, without further ado, ladies and gentlemen, Mr. Curtis Jordan."

While standing at the bottom of the stairs leading up to the stage, Curtis looked back to ask, "A, yo, Mr. Wilder. I've been meaning to ask you, how did you convince my dad to let me come back to the class?"

Due to time constraints, Mr. Wilder rushed to answer with a quick response. "*How* I did it isn't as important as *why* I did it. As an outsider, I could see that you and your father wanted the same thing, which was whatever was best for you. As a father, what you must understand is that we can only teach you what we know. Your father knows success through the military. He pushes you in that direction, because he knows that you can have the same success, as opposed to struggling to find your own path. You can't knock him for doing that. Trust me. I'm 100 percent sure that he loves you. Or else he wouldn't care what you did with your life."

"Thanks, Mr. Wilder. I needed to hear that."

"You're welcome. Now, is there any way that I can get you to take those ridiculous looking shades off?"

Curtis smiled. "Not a chance."

Curtis took the stage as people sat. "A, yo. First off, I want to thank y'all for the award and everything. *But* don't think for one second that I didn't notice how y'all ain't give me that extra $20,000." The audience laughed. "I know I ain't win in my category, so I ain't trippin' about it. But I don't want y'all to think y'all slick, either." The audience laughed again. "Now, I want to thank my mother, who I love dearly, and who has been wonderful to me unconditionally." The audience applauded. "But next to her, I would like to thank a man who has seen me grow from a boy to a young man. He has stood by my side, lifted me up, and broke me down as needed. And he has always believed in me. That man is none other than Officer Gary Timmons." The audience applauded again.

Curtis Sr. slapped the back of the chair in front of him. Curtis glanced down at Mr. Wilder, who stood at the bottom of the stairs. "Finally, I would like to get one thing straight. My name is Curtis Jordan Jr. My father, Curtis Sr., and I don't always see eye to eye. But thanks to some new people in my life who've taught me some things, I'm able to see that he loves me and wants nothing but the best for me. Pops, if you're listening, I just want you to know that I genuinely love you too, and I want the same exact thing. *But* now that I got this scholarship, I ain't going to no ROTC on Monday! And that's just all there is to it! I'll holla at y'all."

The audience gave a final round of applause. Curtis chucked up a deuce while stepping out from behind the podium.

Coming down the aisle near his seat, Curtis was attacked with a bear hug from his father.

"I love you so much, Son. And I'm so proud of you. I apologize for not supporting you in this. I wish I would've done more to help."

"It's cool. I love you too, Dad. Besides, you've already done plenty to help. You taught me work ethic, how to manage my money, and a little self-defense every now and then." Curtis playfully jabbed his dad's shoulder. "And a bunch of other things that I use on a daily basis. So don't worry, Dad. I haven't forgotten the morals and values you've taught me."

With tears in his eyes, Curtis Sr. smiled and kissed his son's forehead before giving him another back-cracking hug. Curtis Sr. then turned to face Officer Timmons.

"And thank you, sir, for being where I should've been."

Officer Timmons shook his hand. "I know that takes a lot out of a man to say something like that, and even more so from a father about his son. So to that, I'm just going to say you're welcome. The pleasure was all mine, sir."

Samantha spoke as the group took their seats. "We will now be transitioning over to the adult portion of the ceremony, where two lucky writers will receive a $60,000 publishing contract, courtesy of Summit's Creek Publishing House. The next award we will be presenting is for best adult nonfiction."

After the finalists were announced and the winner was revealed, a middle-aged white woman with big curly blond hair and a large leather purse walked on the stage. From her rugged walk, she appeared painfully uncomfortable in her high-heeled shoes. The woman slammed her purse atop the podium and began her acceptance speech. She'd written a book entitled *Quitting Nicotine in the Nick of Time*, a story about how she'd given up smoking cigarettes one night in the gas station parking lot where she usually purchased them, only to find out later that there was an armed robbery going on inside, where the thieves fatally shot everyone in the store. At the end of her speech, proceeding her applause, she reached for her purse but knocked it off the podium. A carton of Newport cigarettes fell out and slid across the stage.

Once the scaffold was cleared, Samantha reapproached the podium. "Ladies and gentlemen, it is now time for this evening's main event, adult fiction." The audience applauded. "And the nominees are: *Creation of Dreams*, written by Michael Adams. This novel follows a young man who has lost everything except his dignity and ability to write. After receiving a little motivation, he conjures up a novel that allows him to put his wildest dreams and most troubling memories on paper. And it allows everyone who reads it to be mesmerized.

"Next, we have *Jazzy Business*, written by Monique Turner, the story of a world-famous jazz musician's fall from fame due to arthritis. This novel details the hurdles faced and disingenuous friends revealed as she attempts to venture into the business realm of jazz music.

"Our final nominee is *Mr. Wilder*, written by DeSean Briggs. This is the story of a middle-aged white man from suburban America teaching three black teenage inner-city boys creative writing and valuable life lessons, all in the midst of a racially tense murder investigation."

Jaylen and Curtis nudged DeSean in excitement. The hostess peeled open the envelope. "And the winner is…wow. This is unbelievable. For the fourth year in a row, Mr. Michael 'Vegas' Adams!"

Mr. Wilder jumped out of his seat, grabbed his cane, and nearly ran to the front. The crowd gave a standing ovation that lasted his entire way to the stage. Jaylen, Curtis, and DeSean ran after Mr. Wilder, but were stopped by Curtis Sr. and Officer Timmons. The two men repetitively told the boys, "Just wait. Let's see what he has to say."

Mr. Jack Summit came from behind the curtains and stood at the top of the stairs to shake Mr. Wilder's hand. Mr. Wilder humbly spoke into the microphone.

"Thank you all so much. I truly appreciate this. God bless you all, and have a good night." He received his second standing ovation as he rushed off the stage and made a beeline for the rear exit door. He used the aisle on the opposite side of the theater to avoid any conflict with his students and their guests.

DeSean was the angriest of them all. He broke away from the group and ran to catch Mr. Wilder. But he was blocked by an overwhelming crowd of fans who were snapping pictures and trying to exit the building themselves.

The lights were set to their brightest illumination, signaling to guests that the ceremony was complete. Mr. Wilder reached the exit and saw Jawbone, the pessimistic janitor, leaning on the door frame. Mr. Wilder attempted to walk past him without speaking. But Jawbone stood erect to block him.

"Well, well, well. If it ain't Michael 'Da Pussy.' I should've known it was you." Jawbone lifted his phone. "Now, stand still and hold up that envelope so I can get a picture of this bullshit."

Mr. Wilder shoved his cane on the floor, forcefully grabbed Jawbone by the collar of his work uniform, and slammed his back into the doorframe. With Jawbone's feet dangling in the air, Mr. Wilder used the thicker part of his forearm to press against his throat and hold him still.

"Good! Now that you know it's me, I expect you to keep your fucking mouth shut! Are we clear on that?" Unable to speak, Jawbone fearfully nodded with bulging eyes. Mr. Wilder rapidly removed his forearm, causing Jawbone to fall to his hands and knees, gasping for air. Mr. Wilder kicked the cell phone out of Jawbone's hand, picking up his cane and using it as a weapon to strike the phone with each word he said.

"The! Sign! Clearly! Says! No! Fucking! Cell! Phones!" The phone shattered. Mr. Wilder busted open the exit door, stormed through the hallway full of cell phones, and disappeared into the brisk winter night.

None of his fans went after him. They apprehensively kept a safe distance based on his recent actions.

———❦———

Near midnight, DeSean burst through the entry door of Mr. Wilder's apartment. He forcefully shut the door behind himself before cutting on all the lights and screaming, "Mr. Wilder! Vegas! Michael Adams! Whatever your goddamn name is. I know you're in here! I saw your car in the parking lot! Where the fuck are you?"

After he checked the kitchen and living area, DeSean pushed the already cracked bathroom door completely open. There was no one in there. He ran to Mr. Wilder's bedroom door to do the same. But the door was locked. DeSean vigorously banged on the door with both fists.

"Open this door right now, motherfucker! And you're going to tell me everything that's going on too! I had to walk an hour to get here from the ceremony! I couldn't even accept a ride because Jaylen or Curtis would've seen your car and knew I was staying here!"

Once DeSean stopped shouting, he heard the familiar sound of Mr. Wilder writing on his typewriter. Before long, the sound of the keys being punched came to an end. Mr. Wilder spoke tranquilly. "DeSean, I know you have a lot of questions. And I understand why you are angry. I will explain everything and answer all your questions tomorrow morning. But first, I need you to get a good-night's rest and calm down. That is not a conversation we can have with you being furious and irate."

DeSean tried to fake it. He took a deep breath and counted to ten.

"Okay. I'm calm now. I don't need to go to sleep. I'm good. You can come on out now so we can have the conversation."

Mr. Wilder's typing continued without a verbal response.

DeSean slapped the door. "Damn! It's like that, Mr. Wilder? I said I'm fucking calm! Open this door so I can find out what the hell is going on!" The crunching of the typewriter went on. DeSean shrugged a shoulder and nodded repetitively. "Okay, cool. I'll wait till the morning. But I ain't fucking going to sleep, though! I'll bet you that!"

DeSean turned the countertop TV on. Due to only one channel coming through clearly, he was forced to watch an infomercial for Sham Wow. DeSean sat up on the couch and watched the overly enthusiastic host. He was doing such a great job, DeSean thought about getting up and cleaning something himself. After a while, though, even with his anger and the host's contagious energy, DeSean inevitably fell asleep.

<hr />

A few hours later, just after sunrise, DeSean woke up from the sound of the bathroom door closing. Still groggy, he wiped the crust from his eyes before realizing what had happened. DeSean jumped off the couch and ran over to open the bathroom door, but it was locked. He lifted his fist to knock on the door and yell for Mr. Wilder. But the shower began to run, and DeSean decided to save his energy.

He noticed the TV had been on all night. So DeSean walked over to turn it off, until he heard the reporter say, "We're live here again at Booker T. Washington High School in Norfolk, Virginia, where you all may recall, Mr. Riley Schmidt, an English teacher here at the school, was found innocent of all charges for the murder of his student, LaVeon Kirkland." DeSean stopped to listen.

"Since the verdict was released, there have been rallies and random acts of violence from the minority community. However, two young men, who have requested to remain nameless, recently started a petition to have Mayor Rich Newman recalled if this case were not reopened for investigation. The two teenage boys, who are also students here at the school, were able to get over one hundred thousand signatures in only a few short days. As of this morning, all eight of Mr. Kirkland's former teachers have been fired from the Norfolk Public School System indefinitely. And Mr. Schmidt has been taken into custody once again. Hundreds have gathered here at the school to hear, firsthand, Mayor Newman's explanation for all of this. Let's listen in as he takes the podium."

Mayor Newman buttoned his suit jacket. He was sweating profusely as he approached the podium, which had eight microphones, in front of the high school's main entry. A full staff of media was on hand, including reporters, photographers, and cameramen. While he repeatedly patted his face with a handkerchief, Mayor Newman nervously stumbled over his words. He was greeted with disheartening boos from the crowd.

"Hi...hi, good people of Norfolk. Um...I would like to start off by saying that I was personally, uh...displeased and unsatisfied with the original verdict in this case." The crowd booed. "Um...I know that it seems as if the petition for my recalling has been the driving force for this reinvestigation. But uh...I can assure you that that couldn't be any further from the truth. Earlier this year, I was the one who approved the purchase of a brand-new $75,000 surveillance system for this school. The footage from those cameras have just been released as evidence. And...that is what has led to the eight teachers being fired, Mr. Schmidt's second arrest, and the reopening of this investigation."

The crowd was unruly. Someone said, "That's bullshit! We asked to see those tapes months ago!"

DeSean even yelled at the TV. "You're lying! Principal Akers gave those surveillance tapes to the police the morning after the murder! She didn't even have a chance to watch them herself!"

Mayor Newman pleaded, "Listen...please know that I share your frustration. But you all must understand that providing that footage as verified evidence can be a long, complicated legal process." The crowd booed again.

A woman shouted from the crowd, "So why in the hell they ain't wait for all the evidence to be verified before they reached a verdict?" The crowd applauded.

While holding his handkerchief, Mayor Newman surrendered both hands in the air. "Okay. No further questions! No further questions! I simply came to personally update everyone on the progress in justice for the death of LaVeon Kirkland!" The crowd booed again. Mayor Newman panicked.

"Now, I'd like to bring to the podium the woman who raised LaVeon Kirkland, his grandmother, Ms. Suzette Kirkland. More commonly known as Mama Kirk."

With tears in her eyes, she was greeted with an applause as she adjusted the microphones downward. Mama Kirk's salt-and-pepper hair was half braided. She wore a white blouse beneath her pea coat and was accompanied by her daughter and Mayor Newman standing on each side.

"I can't lie to y'all peoples. I'm mad right now. My grandson was shot and killed, they done raised the price of my prescription, and now I can't get my niece to come finish my hair. She told me she was going to be to my house at ten o'clock in the morning yesterday to finish my hair. That heffa ain't show up until nine o'clock that night. Had me sittin' up in the house waitin' for her all day. Then, when she got there, she had the nerve to say, '*I don't know how much I'ma be able to finish today. I'm tired.*' I said, 'I don't know what from. You ain't working nowhere. And you better not had been doing somebody else head all day!' Got me up here on public television looking half crazy."

Her daughter nudged her arm. "Anyway, I die stress."

Her daughter leaned in to whisper in her ear, "Mama, it's *digress*."

"No! You digress! I die stress. That means I ain't worried about it no mo'! I done let it go and gave it to Jesus." Her daughter stepped back and rolled her eyes. "But like I was saying, I'm deeply saddened by the loss of my grandson. He was such a good boy. I remember after his mother passed while giving birth to him, I said at the funeral that I would take care of that boy and make sure he had everything he needed to succeed in life. If only his father, my son, were here to see this today. He would be turning over in his cell."

The mayor interrupted her. "Mama Kirk, I think you meant turning over in his grave."

"No. I meant turning over in his cell. He right up there at the prison in Suffolk. He ain't dead!"

DeSean heard the shower turn off. He snatched the cord to yank the TV plug out of the wall before running to the bathroom door.

DeSean pounded. "Hey! It's the morning! Open up the door! I'm ready to talk!"

Mr. Wilder took a long sigh. "Okay. We can talk. But I'm not opening the door, since I see a good-night's rest hasn't brought you any solace."

"You're damn right it didn't! And I told you it wouldn't! I don't lie like you do! Telling me I should open up to people, when your ass is the one who stole my story! You know I needed that money! How in the hell are you going to tell me, one of your students, to stop writing a story? Just so you can turn around and write it yourself, but then lie and say you're writing a self-help book?"

"Even though I'd only jotted a few notes down, I had the idea for that book the first time I saw you. So technically, I was writing it first. And if it's the money you want, just look on top of the refrigerator. There's the $60,000 envelope from last night. You can have it all. That should cover your tuition costs at ODU and leave you with some pocket change. You would still need to get a job and an apartment, though. But I'll tell you this, you're sitting on a best seller with that book you wrote."

"Man, please! I couldn't even win the competition."

"That doesn't mean anything! Trust me! I know a bestselling novel when I read one. Last night I typed some revisions you should make to your characters, Jaylen and Curtis. But after that, I'll teach you how to self-publish *Mr. Wilder*. And then you'll see."

"Don't worry. I'll take that $60,000. But I ain't believing the hype on all that other stuff, though. I'll believe it when I see it. Besides, why'd you even tell us about the competition if you knew there was a chance we'd find out that you'd been lying to us?"

"The only thing I ever lied to you all about is my name. Everything else I ever told you all is true!"

"Speaking of which, what's your real name, anyway? And why did you lie about it?"

"If you want to know the name on my birth certificate, it's Michael Adams. I lied about it because I knew one of you guys could've easily Googled me and found out who I was. I'm not one for a lot of attention, and I was already trying to stay low key. Plus, I didn't want you guys to listen to me because of my fame but, rather, because of the content of my character. And to answer your original question, I didn't mind telling you all about the competition, because I wasn't planning on going. I haven't been able to write a book since my wife left me over fifteen years ago. I just couldn't get inspired about anything. All those books

I'm 'famous' for were written while I was in my twenties. But teaching you guys the art of creative writing and hanging around you all eventually gave me new inspiration to write."

"No! You told me you wrote fifteen books that never got published!"

"That's right. I did. I couldn't get a publisher to touch those fifteen books I wrote in my twenties. Then, as I told you before, I started making some changes, and that's when my wife left me. But I was able to get my first book published. And every year since then, I would just submit one of my old books to the competition. Looking back on it, I can't necessarily say that choosing my passion for writing over the love of my life was the best decision."

"Oh, I get it. You weren't going to go to the competition this year because you'd already submitted all of the books you'd written?"

"Exactly."

DeSean spoke sarcastically. "I guess it's safe to say that you didn't retire from the chicken plant because of wise stock market investments either, huh?"

Mr. Wilder snickered. "Yes, I almost forgot about that lie."

"Wait a minute! If you were so done with writing, why'd you even apply for the job?"

"I really didn't want the job. But I knew it would be a good way to get the information I needed to rescue my stepson. Which is what I originally came here for."

"Stepson? Who the hell is your stepson?"

"You remember Conner from the picture on the desk. In the country, a lot of people go by their middle names. You know him as Mr. Riley Conner Schmidt."

"Hell naw! You ain't rescuing that motherfucker from shit! He's going to get what he deserves!"

"Calm down, DeSean. I've had a change of heart. I've been bailing him out of trouble it seems like his whole life. The truth of the matter is that he's followed in the steps of his biological father. Except he's taken it to another level. That's usually what happens when generational curses aren't properly dealt with. But after I found out he was guilty and why, and I saw the effect this murder had on people, I decided to let him suffer through this one."

"I don't even know why you care, anyway! Mr. Riley's a grown-ass man! And he's just your stepson!"

"I know. But I felt that rescuing him was a way to show my wife that I still loved her and cared for her and her son."

"Ex-wife. But I guess I can understand that. And I will say that if I had to be rescued, you'd be the man I'd want to do it. I saw what you did to Jawbone."

"Yeah. He just got underneath my skin one too many times." The water ran from the sink as Mr. Wilder brushed his teeth.

"Wow. Really! I didn't know he knew you well enough to get under your skin."

"Yeah, well, he's my father."

DeSean's head snapped back in confusion. He didn't think he'd heard Mr. Wilder clearly due to the brushing and the bathroom door, which acted as a sound barrier between the two.

DeSean mumbled, "I'm getting sick of this shit." He grabbed the knob and rammed his shoulder into the door. The lock ripped through the wooden frame. DeSean regained his balance and looked up. Standing at the sink in a towel was a tall, muscular, clean-shaven man with mahogany-brown skin. A lifelike costume resembling a middle-aged Caucasian man hung over the shower rack.

Photo By: Figure This LLC

Shelton R. Johnson is a graduate of James Madison University and a native of Norfolk, Virginia. Before penning *Mr. Wilder*, he wrote and published two comedic novels. Johnson currently lives in Maryland with his wife and two children.

www.ingramcontent.com/pod-product-compliance
Lightning Source LLC
Chambersburg PA
CBHW030918120626
46554CB00001B/203